SAVING SARAH MAY

S.J. REISNER

This is a fictional work. The names, characters, incidents, places, and locations are solely the concepts and products of the author's imagination or are used to create a fictitious story and should not be construed as real.

5 PRINCE PUBLISHING AND BOOKS, LLC
PO Box 16507
Denver, CO 80216 www.5PrinceBooks.com

Print ISBN 13: 978-1-63112-150-0 ISBN 10:1631121502
Saving Sarah May
S.J. Reisner
Copyright S.J. Reisner 2016
Published by 5 Prince Publishing
Front Cover Ermisenda Alvarez

First Edition/First Printing April 2016 Printed U.S.A.
5 PRINCE PUBLISHING AND BOOKS, LLC.

Acknowledgements:

I'd like to give a huge thanks to Connie Kline for her long support of this project. With her encouragement and editorial input *Saving Sarah May* came to be. A huge thanks to 5PP and the entire staff for all their work bringing my debut contemporary romance novel to readers. Thanks also goes to Tanya for patiently listening to me and providing encouragement when I needed it. Finally, a shout out to my street-team. You guys are the best!

Dedications:

For my friends. Without you I am without.

SAVING SARAH MAY

1

Sarah

Sarah still couldn't believe it. Eric wasn't coming back. The spacious four bedroom, two story house they'd bought almost a year ago felt empty and big. Cold, even. This was her final walk- through before she, Emily, and Kate left for Ireland, and the house went on the market. The realtor assured her there would be offers by the time she got back. It was a seller's market and she'd heard some houses were getting as many as forty offers in the first forty- eight hours. Sarah would easily get enough money to put a down payment on the two-bedroom condominium she planned to move to.

Stifling an unbidden sob, she brought her hands to her eyes and wiped the tears away, and then laughed when she realized she'd just walked through the kitchen, dining room, and living room practically in the dark. That's how it had been lately. Crying then laughing, or from laughing to crying. She couldn't control it. Outside, the sun drew further behind the mountains.

Flipping on the lights in the living room, her eyes fell on the silver framed photograph of Eric in full dress uniform. She kept telling herself she would take it down, like she had all the others, and put it in one of the boxes with the rest of his things in the garage, but she couldn't. Taking down the picture would somehow make it final, and she wasn't ready for that. They had plans, real plans. She already had her ad agency and he was going to start his own auto repair shop. They'd already decided to start trying for a baby that summer. Now none of that would happen.

She went over to the picture and traced her finger along the frame, seeing his face through tear-filled eyes. A face she'd never see again. Shaking her head, she didn't want to make his death final.

But it is final, she scolded herself. *Eric is dead, Sarah. Get a grip.*

Now, the tears flowed freely down her cheeks and she didn't try to hold them back. It had been five months and it still felt like mere days. The Army didn't send informal letters to tell you when someone died. No, they sent grim men in formal uniforms to deliver the news personally.

Being that Eric didn't have any real family except her, they showed up at her door on a Thursday evening, and when they did, she knew he was gone before they said anything. The Army wouldn't have made a house call otherwise.

She remembered one of the men saying something about a bomb, and that Eric died instantly. Distantly she heard her own voice wail, "Oh God, no."

Then she collapsed into one of the men's arms, inconsolable. Her sobs had been so loud, in fact, that her crying summoned Mrs. Hughes from next door. The graying, portly woman, dressed in a neatly pressed house dress and apron as if she'd just walked out of a fifties movie, stayed with her during those initial crying jags, holding her close until Kate could arrive. She didn't remember how long it took for Kate to get there, but when she did, she immediately dropped her purse next to the couch and she and Mrs. Hughes switched places, replacing Mrs. Hughes softer frame with Kate's thin and bony one. She remembered thinking briefly, through shattered tears, that Mrs. Hughes was nicer to lean against, but she wasn't picky.

Kate stayed with her for three weeks after that, getting breaks from Emily, until both of her best friends were reasonably certain she could be left alone. The funeral was a blur and she didn't remember much, except that she was numb and an endless torrent of people passed by her, giving her their condolences and telling her that only time could ease the pain. So far it hadn't. Not one bit. It was Em and Kate who sent the thank you notes to everyone and took care of everything those weeks afterward while she moped around the house like a zombie. Claire and Ben ran the office that first month afterward, and when Sarah was ready, she went back to work and realized that when working, she wasn't thinking about Eric or how happy they'd been.

It was no wonder the last quarter was the agency's most profitable so far. Work Sarah could manage. Life alone in a big, empty house was another story altogether. Kate kept telling her to get back to living, and that Eric wouldn't have wanted her to mourn forever. Logically, she knew Kate was right, but there was no room for logic in emotions.

Sarah figured Kate's suggestion that the three of them go to Ireland for three weeks in May was a last ditch effort to pull her out of her grief, but even she wasn't sure it would work. As far as she was concerned, her life was over. Life without Eric meant nothing. No future, no children.

Nothing.

While Kate tried to encourage Sarah, Emily took a different approach. Em, a pragmatic mother of one and recently divorced, didn't mince words when Sarah tried to talk herself out of going on the trip. Emily told her straight up, "Look, Sarah, I know you're hurting, but you have to get back into the world. Eric died and that's horrible and painful and it sucks, but life goes on. Kate and I are here for you, but we want to be here for you in Ireland, so say yes and let Kate buy the tickets already."

With a weak laugh and a forced smile, she'd agreed. How could she refuse that kind of pragmatic thinking?

Now, she just felt sad. Sad knowing that she would go on this trip with her friends and Eric would still be gone. When she returned, the house would likely be as good as sold. Once the house sold, that was really *it*.

She picked up the framed picture of Eric and pulled it to her, swallowing back another sob. Holding it close, she went to the garage and opened the door, flicking on the light. There, stacked neat in the corner, stood Eric's boxes. Sucking in a ragged breath, and with tears still falling, she forced herself to the nearest box, opened it, and gently set the picture inside, on top. Closing the box she wiped her eyes again and went back into the house.

"Okay," she consoled herself. "Everything is going to be okay."

With that, she went through the downstairs one last time to make sure the house looked presentable for potential buyers and the open house on Sunday.

"I can do this. Today is a new beginning," she told herself as she came back to the foot of the stairs. After making sure the front door was locked, she went up to her bedroom to finish packing. Maybe Kate and Em were right. She wanted to get away and this trip was exactly what she needed.

2

Emily

"Mom, do you need hair bands?" Lucy, twelve going on thirty, poked her blonde head and one hand into the room, wiggling a handful of colored hair bands.

"Oh, a few of those might be good." Emily reached out and took them from her daughter. "Thank you. Now you know that you still have to do your homework when I'm not here, right? No matter what your dad or your grandmother say."

"I'm not allowed to do homework at Dad's because Cheri wants Dad's house to be the *fun* house. I'll do it in study hall." The long-legged pre-teen flopped herself onto the bed next to the open suitcase. "Do you need a hair dryer?"

Emily ignored the mention of Cheri, the twenty-six-year- old school teacher Sam had dumped her for. It still stung. "No, I think the cottage comes with a hair dryer and towels."

"Why aren't you guys staying in a hotel?"

"The cottage was cheaper and it's more fun," she said with a smile. While she hated leaving Lucy, she needed to get away. It had been a rough year. After losing her house in the divorce and Sam pretty much handing over custody of Lucy, except overnight visits every other weekend, she needed the break. Even more, Sarah needed her. There she went again - focusing on Sarah and Lucy to keep her mind off of Sam and Cheri. At this point, she was sure Lucy and Sarah were the only reasons she was still sane.

Cheri, according to Sam, made him feel young again and she was far more outgoing and social than Emily ever had been. Not to mention thinner. That was good news for Sam. Now he finally had the trophy girlfriend, soon-to-be-wife, he'd always wanted. Cheri would look pretty attached to his arm during city and political social events. The problem with Sam was everyone he worked with loved him, and he'd risen to the position of city manager rather easily. But he was emotionally abusive, manipulative, and a first class jerk when no one was watching. Emily didn't envy Cheri that. It was the emotional abuse that made the divorce easier.

Cheri would figure it out soon enough when her looks started to falter or she gained ten pounds, whichever happened first. That's how it was with Sam. In the beginning, everything had been fine, but then things changed. In public, they'd been the picture perfect family. He loved her, she loved him, and they had a beautiful daughter together. Behind closed doors he constantly yelled at Lucy for whatever reason, and told Emily how worthless she was. He'd even bitched about her weight and requested she change her hair color so she would look *presentable* in public. When she refused, he went out and found Cheri.

"What are you forgetting?" Lucy asked, pulling Emily from bitter memories that set her jaw on edge.

"I just don't know what I'm preparing for here," she lied and looked at the suitcase.

Lucy shrugged. "Rain? I read on the internet that it rains in Ireland. A lot. Especially in the spring. That's why it's so green."

"Well, I have the rain jacket. I just don't know if I need something formal."

The twelve-year-old had an answer for everything. "The fanciest place will probably be a pub. If you need anything fancier, I'm sure they have dress shops."

She shook her head and smiled at her daughter. "You're absolutely right. When did you get so smart, huh?"

Lucy gave her mother a bright smile. "Will you send me a lot of pictures?"

"Every day I'll email you pictures and tell you what I did."

"Promise?"

"Of course."

"Can I have Leslie over one night when you're gone?"

"Ask your grandmother. It's up to her. Or maybe you can go to her house when you're at your dad's?"

"Nah, that would make him and Cheri happy. If I'm going to be a burden, I plan on being one with pride."

Emily fought back a laugh. "Well then ask your grandmother."

"Okay."

"Give me a hug."

"Can't you hug me tomorrow? It's not like I'm not seeing you in the morning before you go."

Sitting on the bed next to her, she scooped Lucy into her arms and hugged her anyway, even though she was almost as tall as her mother. "I'm going to miss you."

"I'll miss you, too. But Grandma and I will be fine. We've already planned wild Friday nights filled with gin rummy. It's a plus I only have to spend one night at Dad's while you're gone."

Emily eased up on her embrace and gave Lucy a knowing look. "You know your dad loves you despite everything, right?"

"Yeah," she said with a resigned sigh. Lucy seemed to take the divorce in stride. She was a smart girl. She knew what was going on.

"I still don't understand the ban on homework. What kind of fun things does Cheri suppose you'll do?" Fighting back a snort, she rolled another blouse to put in her suitcase.

"You mean when they don't drop me off at a friend's or leave me with the old neighbor lady who has like *five* cats?"

Emily kept the smart-ass remark that came to mind to herself. "Yeah, when you guys *actually* spend time together."

"Usually we rent a movie on pay-per-view because Dad's too cheap to take us to a *real* movie. And they're always dumb movies that I don't want to watch, like romantic comedies." Lucy stuck out her tongue and scrunched up her nose.

"Well, next time you should suggest a movie you want to watch." She shrugged. "Make them do something that's fun for you once in a while."

Lucy snorted then said, in the snottiest voice Emily had ever heard her daughter use, "What Cheri wants, Cheri gets."

With a cringe and a head shake, she took an inventory of her toiletry bag. "Toothpaste."

Lucy jumped up and sprinted into the bathroom. "I'll get it."

The scent of pot roast drifted from somewhere downstairs. Just as quickly as Lucy returned with the toothpaste, she disappeared like a feral animal in search of the source, mumbling something about being *really* hungry. There would be no more talk of Sam and Cheri tonight.

Emily took a deep breath and kept packing. The memory of Sam's mental abuse and his infidelity still hurt even now. Even though she knew she and Lucy were better off. When he broke her heart, she vowed never to give her heart to another man, and she didn't regret that promise one bit. Truthfully she didn't need a man to survive. She had everything she needed. A wonderful daughter, great friends, supportive family, a good job at the bank, and plenty of goals and dreams to lead a full, prosperous life.

Perspective. That's what she needed. Three weeks in Ireland was sure to give her that. Besides, it would be good for Sarah, and the reality was - this trip was all about helping Sarah deal with Eric's death.

3

Kate

How could Lisa do this to her? Her own sister?! Kate almost threw the phone but stopped herself. Instead, she set the phone down and picked up a stack of cooking magazines and threw them against the wall. It was hardly satisfying, and now she had to clean it up. She drew in a deep breath and regained her composure. She wasn't going to cry - that would be stupid. After all, she'd only been dating Josh Stevens for a month. That was hardly enough time to develop feelings for him. Nonetheless, she was pissed. How dare Josh go after Lisa, her own sister! And how dare her sister say *yes*! Grabbing the throw pillow next to her, she pulled it to her face and screamed into it, howling with rage.

It was times like this she wished she had a punching bag so she could imagine it was Josh's face. Or Lisa's. This wasn't the first time her sister had gone out with one of her boyfriends. Lisa's only excuse; "Oh, I didn't know you were still dating. He told me you weren't exclusive..."

"Ugh!" Unclenching her fists, she looked at the nail marks in her palms, then quickly inspected the manicure she'd gotten just that afternoon. That manicure had to last at least half way through Ireland. This couldn't have been worse timing. She still had to pack and it was already nine. In nine hours the taxi would arrive to pick her up. Then they'd wind their way through the early morning streets to pick up Emily and Sarah. It would take at least an additional forty minutes to an hour to get to the airport depending on traffic, and then two hours to get through security. That left them plenty of time to have breakfast at the airport before heading to their gate. The plane left in fifteen hours, which gave her only an hour to put a bag together if she wanted to get at least eight hours of sleep. She could never sleep on the plane.

Taking a deep breath, she closed her eyes and tried to find her center. That's what she needed. Yoga. Maybe a half hour of yoga would get her in the mood to pack. Besides, Lisa and Josh were bound to be broken up by the time she returned from her trip. That thought satisfied her more than it should have. She knew Lisa well enough to know that she always coveted Kate's boyfriends. Lisa would go after them, sleep with them, and get dumped over and over again. Likewise, it wasn't that Kate didn't know Josh was a dog, too, she just hoped he wouldn't be a dog to her. Same story, different guy. She always went after the bad boy. It wasn't intentional, she just wasn't attracted to the stable, loyal, responsible types. They were boring. The players fit in with her lifestyle, certainly. But that didn't make her immune to the jealousy she always felt every time one of them dumped her for a new piece of ass.

"Maybe you shouldn't be giving away the milk for free," Emily, always told her, then added, "Make them work for it."

It wasn't that Kate didn't want them to work for it. She just didn't want anything to get serious. After all, she'd seen her friends get serious about men and where had it gotten them? Sarah was an emotional wreck with a shattered heart and Emily's heart did her surname, Frost, justice. Unlike them, her heart was still free and undamaged, and she intended to keep it that way.

That still didn't help the seething jealousy and anger she felt. She took another deep breath as she put down the yoga mat, stepped onto it, and moved into tree pose.

Focusing on her breath, she began her sun salutations. It seemed appropriate since she was trying to regain a positive, energetic mindset. Sarah was counting on her. The fact was that both of her friends needed this trip more than she did. That's why she'd suggested it.

For Sarah, Kate felt it was an important part of the grieving process to remove her from the familiarity of her grief. Whereas Emily just needed some time away. Being a single mom was beginning to wear on Em, and Kate could see it in the weary look of Em's green eyes. For Kate - this trip was all about fun, and work. She figured they'd hit a few hot Irish dinner spots while they were out there so she could write up reviews for several of the magazines and newspapers she wrote for. Of course, no one ever could tell the blonde, slender thirty-one-year-old was a well-known food critic. She kept herself in shape and ate sensibly. Plus she was blessed with a high metabolism. All things most women in their thirties envied.

Yes, this trip was going to be great and she just knew that once Sarah was away from that house and Emily was free from twenty- four-seven responsibility, they would both have a great time. The cottage she rented was a perfect three bedroom with a thatched roof, wi-fi, state of the art television, and a full kitchen so they could make their own food if they wanted to. It was centrally located in County Galway, by the bay. Close enough to the ocean, and close enough to shops and restaurants while still having that old world feel to it. That feeling of seclusion and being able to get away from it all. It was perfect and the owner had even given them a discount when Kate explained that they were trying to help Sarah through her grief after losing her fiancé. He seemed to think that was a noble reason to take the trip and insisted that if there was anything they needed, anything at all, he would help them out in any way he could. Nice folks, the Irish.

Four sun salutations later she felt her optimism and positivity returning. Nothing mattered except the trip. Josh and Lisa were like a bad memory from the past. She was ready to move forward. When she finished her set of ten sun salutations, she put the mat away, took another deep, cleansing breath, and went into the bedroom of her small one-bedroom apartment to pack. The excitement began brewing in her stomach. In less than fourteen hours, she and her closest friends would be off on *the best* vacation ever.

4

Away

Emily waved to Lucy one last time as the cab pulled away from the curb and started down the street.

"So Josh dumped me." Kate's voice sounded dejected.

It was the same song and dance all over again. Emily had heard this story at least five times now, maybe six. "Who did you catch this one screwing?"

She let out a heavy sigh, disappointed that she was so transparent. "My sister."

"Again?" Emily groaned. "You keep going out with the *wrong* kind of guy. Of course, I'm one to talk."

"Is it just that all men are jerks?" Kate frowned. When she did, she looked much older than her thirty-one years. The frown made her cheeks fall, and her eyes looked tired.

Of course, the tired eyes could have also been the result of too much partying, Emily mused.

With a shrug, Emily said, "I think I married an ass, and I think you date jerks. But I still have faith there are good men out there. Just not for *me*."

"Ooh!" started Kate with a huge grin. "Maybe we'll meet some nice Irish men."

Laughter tumbled from Emily's throat. "And she's back on the horse, ladies and gentlemen!"

"I didn't call Sarah this morning. You don't think maybe she forgot do you?" Kate seemed suddenly worried.

Running a hand through her long brown hair, Emily shook her head. "She did *not* forget."

Sarah had been through so much more than both of them. If Emily could have, she would have given Sam's life for Eric's. The gruesome thought made her laugh, but then she remembered that Sam was still Lucy's dad, and despite all his faults, Lucy loved him. She let out a heavy sigh. "Just remember, no talking about Eric. It's not that we want her to forget him, but we don't want her to dwell on him either."

Kate nodded absently as the cab pulled up to Sarah's driveway. The *For Sale* sign in the yard said it was a *must see*. From the outside, it looked like a tomb. Of course that could have been the gray day, but there from the curb, it didn't even feel like anyone was home.

Opening the cab door, Kate jumped out. "I'll go get her."

Before she reached the steps leading to the porch, the door opened and out came Sarah with her travel bag and one suitcase. That was Sarah, always practical and packing light.

"Do you need help?" Emily called from the car. "I've got it," she called back with a forced smile. Her dark brown eyes looked haunted.

The cab driver popped the trunk and got out, helping the women put Sarah's luggage with the rest. Once they were all loaded into the back of the cab, they were on their way to the airport.

Now that Kate had her friends' full attention she pulled out her notes. While she may have sucked at picking men, she could organize a trip like nobody's business. "So, we arrive at the Shannon airport what will effectively be tomorrow, at ten in the morning Ireland time. I have a car already reserved. We head straight to our cottage to unpack. I have read that jet lag is possible. The good news is we're within walking distance of the ocean, two small towns, and our cottage's caretaker lives in the house up the road if we find we need anything. But the cottage has full amenities."

"I have a whole list of restaurants and pubs I want to check out. My editor is so excited." She was so busy studying her pages that she didn't notice the look Sarah and Emily exchanged.

"Kate," Emily interrupted.

Kate kept babbling. "Oh, and Sarah, you're going to love this — horseback riding right down the road. There's a stable where you can rent horses."

"I brought paddock boots and a pair of breeches. Are one of you going to come riding with me?" Sarah's full lips contorted into a pout.

Emily raised an eyebrow. "I don't think so…"

Kate didn't respond. She simply kept going through her notes.

"Kate," Em tried again to interrupt.

"Well just in case you need anything or your luggage gets lost - I checked, they have boots and helmets you can borrow, or you can just go to the riding shop in town and get what you need there. I mean theoretically you could go riding every day if you wanted," Kate said.

Emily tried again. "Kate!"

"Huh?" She acted like she had no idea her friend had been trying to get her attention. This trip was just so exciting and more than anything, she wanted Sarah to relax. Even if she forgot about Eric for only a few minutes, it would have been better than nothing.

"We're going to have hours and hours of travel time to discuss this. Can we just relax on our ride to the airport? I don't know about you guys, but I didn't sleep much last night, which means if I want to sleep, I am going to have to catch it in the cab and on the plane." She closed her eyes.

"Well, you can sleep. Sarah and I can talk about all of the cool things there are to do." She nodded at Sarah, continuing. "And you know what? No schedule just like you guys said. We can do what we want when we want. Or, if you don't feel like doing anything, you can stay at the cottage and watch television in bed all day."

Emily's eyes flew open and she gave Kate a warning look. "No one is spending this holiday in bed. We're going to go out, get some fresh air, see Ireland, and do things.

Gain new cultural perspective."

"You guys, I really appreciate what you're trying to do," Sarah said, "But I'm okay. I'm not going to spend the entire day laying around the cottage being all depressed and mopey. I promise, okay? Besides, horseback riding sounds fun. Thanks for checking into that for me, Kate."

Emily put her arm around her friend of twelve years. "We know. We just want you to have a good time. Life has had more bad than good lately."

Sarah gave her a bright smile, with those sad, haunted eyes of hers. "Well, what doesn't kill us makes us stronger."

"Oh God, great, thank you, now I have Kelly Clarkson stuck in my head," Kate groaned.

Her friends laughed. That was Kate. Always the joker.

The rest of the ride to the airport consisted of Kate telling them about Josh and her sister, and Emily avoiding the topic of Sam by doting on Lucy. Sarah just smiled and listened. She had nothing left to add. There was no way she planned on talking about work. Besides, she liked listening to Kate and Em's adventures and problems. In some sick and twisted way, it made her feel better that everyone's life could get difficult and fill with problems. But like usual, Kate was already looking forward to meeting new men and Emily was looking forward to the vacation. Being a single mom had been hard on her. Probably harder than the divorce itself, especially since Sam was a misogynist. Emily was better off without him and both Kate and Sarah knew it.

The Denver airport was a mad house. They still had to fly to Newark and take an international flight from there. After checking bags and grabbing breakfast to take on the plane, they made it to their gate in time to board their first flight. Emily worked puzzles, Sudoku were her favorites. Kate read several fashion magazines she brought, and Sarah tried to immerse herself in the latest bestseller. By the time the flight landed in Newark, all three of them could feel the hours of travel taking their toll. Kate had made sure the layover was four hours, long enough for them to navigate the airport and reach their next flight with ease. When they finally boarded the Aer Lingus flight to Shannon, Ireland, nonstop, all three breathed a sigh of relief. Sarah downloaded another book just in case, Emily bought a novel and another puzzle book, and Kate stocked up on magazines. It wasn't that they didn't want to talk to each other during the flight, just that there was only so much to say about the trip. They'd been planning it for months already. It seemed pointless to prattle on like school girls.

Each of them had her own idea of the things she wanted to do. Sarah wanted to go horseback riding and walk through quaint towns. Perhaps even stroll a beach. Of course, sightseeing wasn't out of the question. Kate's primary interest was the local cuisine. She had plans for every meal, with backup plans just in case the first plan didn't go through. If she played her cards right, she'd be able to get at least seven articles out of this trip, and that would pay for the trip twice over. Of course, it also made the trip a business expense that she could write off on her taxes. Emily wanted to stroll the beaches and go sightseeing. She already had a list of places she wanted to visit and knew some of them would require the car since they were a bit southwest of where they were staying. The Burren, the Cliffs of Moher, and an eleventh-century cathedral tour were all on her list. The plan had never been to do everything together on this trip, but to do their own thing during the day, unless one of the others wanted to come along, and then get together in the evening for carefully planned dinner outings orchestrated by Kate. If Kate knew anything, she knew food, so her friends knew they could count on never starving when they were with her. Surprisingly she didn't do much cooking herself despite the numerous subscriptions to cooking magazines.

The long flight also offered them time to reminisce about their college days, where they'd met. They shared a small apartment just off campus. Emily was the oldest, now thirty- four, and she'd been a senior. Kate, now thirty-one, was a sophomore at the time, and Sarah was a year younger. It was her first year at college and the only reason she didn't stay on campus in a dorm with the rest of the freshmen was because they ran out of room and allowed a small handful of freshmen to find off-campus housing. The three of them lived in that apartment together for two years until Emily met Sam and got pregnant with Lucy, which was the only reason they got married to begin with.

The women laughed over fond memories of the strange grilled cheese experiments they'd done in the tiny galley kitchen, and how they insisted all of their sandwiches were gourmet panini.

By the time the plane landed, they were all tired and uncomfortable and thankful to be off the plane and in Ireland.

"Wow. This is the tiniest airport ever," Kate said, looking straight down to the sign labeled baggage claim. People whizzed past them, intent on their destinations. No one seemed to notice three American women who were bewildered by the small airport and the lack of crowds. The baggage claim was a different story. The entire plane waited around the carousel until the bags came through. Unlike in American cities where people pushed and shoved, grabbing bags unapologetically, not minding their manners, the people here were polite and waited their turn, even if the luggage had to go around a second time.

Once they'd navigated the throng of people, they found the car rental counter, and after twenty minutes and plenty of paperwork, Kate had secured a car. A red Volkswagen Golf. She took the driver's side with a strong bravado.

"Do you think you'll be okay driving on the left?" Emily seemed genuinely nervous.

Sarah giggled.

"Thanks for your unwavering faith in me." After they were all settled and buckled in, she started the car, opened her GPS on her phone, and pulled from the parking space. "I studied the map for a bit on the plane, and it looks like an easy shot to Kilnook. Everyone ready?"

Without waiting for an answer, she pulled from the parking lot, and in a few minutes they were on the M18 heading north.

"This is so incredible. I can't even believe we're in another country," Emily said. It was the first time she'd ever been out of the States.

"It's not as humid as I thought it might be," Sarah said. "When I went to the Bahamas with my grandmother when I was fifteen, it was so humid. I remember one day it rained and the rain was warm. It felt like standing in a shower. I guess I just thought all islands were *that* humid. Probably not this far north."

"So many shades of beautiful green, though," Emily said, trying to take a few photos on her phone through the open passenger side window.

"Everything is so modernized and sponsored by the same corporations nowadays you can't tell one developed country from another except for language," said Kate.

Kate's job took her all over the world, and yet this was her first time in Ireland. One of her biggest pet peeves were the big chain restaurants that one could find in every city in America. It was only a matter of time before the rest of the civilized world was besieged by brand-name, corporate fine dining establishments. One could already see it happening with fast food and coffee chains.

The time passed quickly with small talk and observations of the scenery. When they got to Gort, they switched to N18. Kate already had the directions firmly embedded in her brain. She'd only looked them over a hundred times it seemed. If the map on her phone was right, the cottage would be just inside County Galway near Kinvarra in a small, allegedly quaint Irish town called Kilnook. So far the drive had only taken about an hour with traffic and by her estimation they'd be there soon.

It was good to see Sarah enjoying herself and Kate hadn't seen Sarah smile this much in a long time.

5

The Cottage

At first it wasn't apparent where the cottage was.

They'd gotten off the main road onto a narrow dirt road that led up a hill through tunnels of trees in shades of green ranging from celadon to sage.

Since Kate had done a fantastic job driving on what Emily deemed *the wrong side of the road*, Sarah and Emily sat back and enjoyed the scenery. Something about the entire place had lulled them into a relaxed stupor, or perhaps it was just the jet lag.

Finally, they saw a large, modern ranch style house to their left with a long circular drive out front.

Kate pulled into the driveway, around to the front door and put the car in park, and then studied her map for a moment. Then she looked at a sheet of paper she pulled out of her bag. "This can't be right."

Emily immediately panicked. "Don't tell me you don't know where we're going…"

"Relax, Em, I got this." She got out of the car and went straight up to the house. After ringing the doorbell, Kate turned back to the car and gave them a quick thumbs up, then turned back to the door just as six foot of handsome answered. He had broad shoulders and dark hair, and looked as though he hadn't shaved in about a day. No older than thirty-five, he wore jeans and a plain black t-shirt.

While Sarah barely gave him a second glance, Emily

strained to give him a better look. "What if he's a mass murderer?"

Sarah glanced out the window at Kate and the attractive stranger. He was pointing further down the road. "Doubtful."

"Are you an expert in mass murderers?"

"Yes, and he's not one. Mass murderers aren't usually good looking." With a shrug, Sarah sighed and focused her attention on a flock of sheep in the pasture across the way.

With a laugh, Emily shook her head. "Serial killers look just like anyone else."

The man with Kate disappeared into the house and Kate stayed on the porch as if she were waiting for something. He emerged a few minutes later and handed her an envelope and a set of keys. Then they exchanged some words and smiles and he waved at the car, nodded at Kate, and disappeared inside.

Kate returned with a smile and got into the car, handing the envelope and keys to Emily. "This is it. It is down the hill on this road."

"That guy and his wife run the place?" Emily sounded disappointed.

"He and his mom do," said Kate, pulling around the drive back to the road.

"Norman Bates anyone?" Emily's voice was flat. Sarah laughed.

"What?" Kate glanced at Emily.

"Guy in his thirties, rents out a small carriage house, lives with his mom…" Emily tried to lead a confused Kate into her line of thinking.

"Em thinks that guy is a serial killer." Sarah burst out laughing again.

Kate shook her head. "Doubtful."

The road went up a bit more and curved to the right, going downhill slightly. On the right, a drive led down to the cottage. Beyond the small house, they had a breathtaking view of the surrounding fields, and in the distance, it looked like a lake, perhaps even an ocean inlet.

"Wow," came Sarah's surprised voice from the backseat. "Kate, this is incredible!"

Emily rubbed her arms to brush away the chill of excitement that washed over her. "I have to take a picture of this and send it to Lucy and mom."

With a proud smile, Kate nodded her head once. "I am more than just a pretty face, you know."

She put the car in park and they all got out and took in the fragrant air and shades of olive and moss. The house, while halfway down the hill, faced out over the mountains. It was a clear day and everything stood out vibrantly against the sun-filled sky. In the distance one could see the ocean, its surface glistening with sunlight.

"I think we're seeing every hue of green imaginable," Sarah said. Then her thoughts went to Eric and how he would have loved this. She was able to fight back the tears before they came by shoving the thought into that dark place at the back of her mind.

"I suppose this might be why they call it the Emerald Isle," Emily said. She retrieved her phone from her pocket and stepped forward to get a good picture. The picture hardly did it justice. Surprisingly the phone was getting good reception now, and she was able to send it to her mother's phone.

Sarah decided to walk around the outside of the dwelling on her own. Being cooped up traveling with Kate and Em had been somewhat exhausting. She just wanted to find a quiet place to sit and meditate. Alone with her thoughts.

Kate winced as she watched Sarah disappear around the back of the building. When she was certain Sarah was out of earshot, she leaned over and whispered to Emily, "Should one of us go with her?"

"What are you afraid she'll do? Throw herself down a hill?" Emily laughed. "She's fine. Give her a few minutes."

"She hasn't been talking much." Kate's eyes darted back and forth at either side of the house, waiting for Sarah to round the corner.

"Maybe she has nothing to say." Emily shrugged and went back to the car to get the luggage out of the trunk. "Did Norman Bates clue you in to the closest grocery store or place to find food? I'm kinda hungry."

"There's a list of restaurants and a map in the envelope.

I'm sure we can find a grocery store in town. And we should call him by his proper name to be polite. His name is Sean. Sean O'Flannigan."

Emily snorted. "Of course it is."

"You're so critical of anyone with a penis."

"I don't care that he has a penis, I just think there's something wrong with a guy who, at his age, isn't married with kids." She hefted two suitcases from the trunk and started toward the door of the cottage.

Kate rolled her eyes behind Emily's back and took two of the cases herself, following her down the path to the doorstep. A smart remark about stereotyping teetered on the edge of her lips, but she thought better of it. There was no way she wanted the trip to start with her and Em arguing.

She let Emily grab the rest of the bags while she fumbled with the key in the door. With a gentle shove she pushed it open, half expecting a musty smell to waft out of the closed up space. Instead, a light, airy floral scent flooded through the open door.

Just then, Sarah came back around the side of the house. "Oh, you guys should have waited. I just wanted to see the view from the back. It's great, you should go look while I take the luggage inside."

Emily grabbed Kate by the hand and practically dragged her along. "I'd like to see it."

Kate didn't argue, she followed along, glancing back at Sarah whose lithe frame lifted two suitcases and disappeared inside. In silence they rounded the side of the cottage and made their way around the back. This view was just as grand, but the rolling hills were even more vibrant back here, or they appeared to be.

"She wasn't kidding." Emily took out her phone again and snapped another picture. It was probably the middle of the night back home, but at least Lucy and Mom would wake up to the beautiful photographs.

"We should go back inside," Kate started.

"Kate - relax. I get that you're on a mission to save Sarah from depression, herself, and whatever dismal fate you suspect she'll befall, but really - she's going to be okay. I agree that this trip is a good thing for her, but you can't hover over her. Give her some space." She slipped her phone back into her pocket, closed her eyes, and breathed in the smell of warm spring earth.

"Says the woman who hates all men because she married and divorced a jerk." It just slipped out and while it was true from her perspective, Kate regretted every word the second the snotty remark fell from her lips.

But Emily didn't waver, or get upset at the comment like Kate expected. Instead, she sighed. "I'm sorry if I hurt your feelings. I know you just want to make sure Sarah's okay. So do I, but we can't keep treating her like she's broken or damaged, or if she's left alone for a second that she'll start crying or something. She's a lot stronger than we give her credit for."

Kate nodded and forced a smile. "You're right. I'm sorry."

"And I don't hate men, I'm just wary of their bullshit. You'd be wise to be the same, especially with your track record," Emily said, turning back toward the front door.

With a laugh, Kate followed. "Fair enough. This is going to be the best trip ever."

Sarah appeared from a corridor to the right and there wasn't a suitcase to be seen in the entryway.

"I put the suitcases in the hall outside the bedrooms," she said, pointing down the corridor. "It seems our common rooms and kitchen are here, and the bedrooms are all down this way."

Room by room the three women made their way through the well-kept cottage, marveling at the wood floors and modern appliances. Even the main sitting room had a state-of-the-art flat screen television.

"I was expecting more rustic, but this is really cool," Emily admitted after they investigated the main bathroom and two of the bedrooms. Of course all of them found the setup of the shower a bit odd, but once they'd talked it out, it all made sense. You had to set the temperature with a dial before turning the water on. Kate said she'd seen something similar in a Bed & Breakfast in Scotland once.

Sarah and Kate took the back two bedrooms overlooking the beautiful green hills while Emily took the master bedroom with the en-suite bathroom.

They only took about fifteen minutes to get settled before they found themselves sitting around the dining room table, planning their trip into town for food and supplies. Kate had already decided they should get a quick bite at the local pub first. Sarah and Emily didn't argue.

Instead they all piled back into the rental car and enjoyed more scenery as Kate navigated the road, too slowly for some Irish, as evidenced when they sped around her. No one honked but at least one of the perturbed motorists shouted soundless curses and shook his fist as he passed them. This didn't faze Kate. She continued slow and steady, ignoring them. Finally, the three women found their way into town. Kate even procured a parking spot right outside the pub without too much difficulty. The locals didn't seem to pay too much attention. At most they received a few pleasant smiles from passersby. Undoubtedly wide-eyed tourists were a common occurrence.

The sound of live music drifted out of the pub into the street, causing Kate to smile. "Oh - a band!"

Wherever there was nightlife, there was Kate, always the life of the party. The extrovert of the three, she had more casual acquaintances than most people and always knew where the next party was.

Sarah sighed, resigning herself to a loud dinner. At least the music would keep her awake. She was tired and from the looks of it, Emily felt the same way.

She fell back behind Sarah and let Kate and Sarah go into the pub before her as if the sound of the violin and guitar would somehow ambush her.

There didn't seem to be seating arrangements, so Kate found an open table near the bar and sat down, motioning her friends to join her. A portly bar matron with curly red locks immediately brought over menus.

At first, the woman said something that none of them understood. Her accent was thick. But Kate jumped right in, "We'd like dinner, too, but I'll have a Guinness."

The barmaid nodded and looked expectantly at the other two. "Harp Lager," Sarah said.

Emily pointed at Sarah, knowing she had good taste in beer.

"I'll have the same. Harp Lager."

The woman set the menus on the table, said something about coming back for their order, gave them a polite nod and turned on her heel and left.

If what the band was playing wasn't Irish folk music, then Emily wasn't sure what it was, but it sounded like folk music. She leaned over to Sarah. "This will at least keep me awake."

With a laugh, Sarah nodded. "I was thinking the same thing."

"What?" Kate smiled over the table at them. "Isn't this great?" She was genuinely excited.

Both of her friends just nodded at her.

Emily didn't know if Kate realized just how tired she and Sarah were. While Kate wanted to skid recklessly straight into the night- life of Kilnook, Sarah and Kate wanted to work their way up to being social with the locals. That meant dinner, then maybe getting acquainted with the rental house, then bed. Tomorrow all of them would start their trip properly by getting out and exploring.

"I think I want to check out the local stable tomorrow," Sarah said. "Are you guys sure you don't want to go riding?"

"I'd likely fall off and break my neck," Emily said with a grin.

Kate was too busy people-watching to hear them.

Emily leaned toward Sarah, "I'll probably just take a walk by the beach tomorrow, and maybe check out the shops in town."

Kate heard this time. "Oh yeah, I'm doing some shopping tomorrow, too! You want to come with?"

"I might," said Emily.

Sarah shrugged. "Maybe. But dinner for sure."

"What about lunch?" Kate asked. She wasn't missing a meal.

"Let's just play it by ear," Emily suggested knowing nothing was more stressful than a vacation where every minute was planned and you had to be at a certain place at a certain time. She knew first hand because Sam did that with every vacation they ever took. Every minute was scheduled and when the schedule didn't go as planned, he'd panic and make scathing remarks about how she or Lucy were ruining a perfectly planned event or outing. Little did he know that those vacations weren't fun for her or Lucy. Perhaps he'd find out on his own when Cheri complained, or when Lucy finally let it slip in a moment of hormonal induced teenage insubordination.

With a murmur of agreement, they all watched the band until the woman came back to take their order.

They all decided on fish and chips just to get it out of the way. While Kate saw the dish as more of a British thing, she liked it and never skipped it when she was in this part of the world. Emily and Sarah simply followed suit. Emily because it sounded easy, and Sarah because she just wanted to eat and get some sleep. The jet lag made her feel woozy.

Two hours later they were back at the cottage, full and enjoying the silence. Sarah and Emily went to bed, and for once, Kate didn't argue.

6

First Ride

The horse was a bay mare about fifteen-two hands. She had a patch of white on her chest, and white on three of four fetlocks.

"Her name is Stella," the young stable hand named Brid said, pushing a stringy strand of blonde hair from her face. "You sure you want to go alone? I can come out with you."

The girl seemed wary about Sarah's experience with horses. Chances are most tourists wanted a guide. Sarah just wanted to go for a ride. No one and nothing except her, the horse, and nature. Eric never liked horses that much. Last year, on his last leave, they'd taken a two day riding trip in the Rocky Mountains, but he hated it and only did it because she wanted to go. She remembered how he'd said, *That can't be fun for the horse. I don't think that's normal. People riding horses. It's weird.*

She shoved the memory away and focused on Stella, petting her velvet nose. "Thanks, Brid, but I think I can handle it."

Turning Stella away, she walked the horse about ten steps then checked the girth. Sure enough, Stella had been holding air and the girth was loose. She re-tightened it, pulling the buckles up another notch, then slid three fingers under the girth to make sure it wasn't too tight.

"Now isn't that better?" she asked the mare, whose only response was to prick her large ears toward Sarah's voice. Starting on the right side, Sarah pulled the stirrup down and adjusted it to make sure it was as long as her arm. Then she went to the left side of the horse and did the same thing. Once she was sure everything was situated she mounted and checked to make sure everything was in order. It was. With that she urged the horse forward with her heels and headed away from the stable, through a meadow, to a horse path that led through shamrock colored fields and deep forests and eventually down to the beach if she wanted to ride that far. Or at least that's where the path led according to Brid, who seemed disappointed she wouldn't get to go for a long ride today.

It wasn't until she was two fields over and the stable was out of range that Sarah began to relax. She could feel the strong withers moving beneath her. Stella seemed to be enjoying the walk as much as Sarah enjoyed riding her. She leaned forward in the saddle and urged the mare into a brisk trot and found the wind on her face freeing and invigorating. Nothing existed except Sarah and Stella and the trail ahead. To her left, high up on the hill, two grand manor houses stood looking out over the hillside. The forest path before them looked dark and foreboding, but Sarah knew it was just her imagination. There were no trolls or faeries hiding amongst the dense trees and deep pine, lush underbrush. Once they reached the forest path and the canopies of trees above cut out most of the sunlight, she slowed Stella to a walk, finding the horse's methodic hoof falls calming. She could understand how fantasies of elves, imps, and other creatures may have come about. The thick underbrush, some of it soft and mossy, looked like something out of a fairytale.

The air under the trees was cool and the scent of the earth stronger and ripe. "So pretty, isn't it Stella?"

Stella's ears flicked back, then forward again.

Sarah didn't want to trot through the forest. The path here was harder and she wasn't sure of the terrain up around the bend, so she decided not to go faster than a walk until she knew the path better. It was probably good she hadn't because for the next mile, the path wound around and up the side of the hill until it emerged on a bright green knoll overlooking more fields and the ocean beyond.

Slipping her phone out of her pocket, she snapped a few photos of the view, then she put it away and dismounted. She could ride to the ocean today if she wanted. Instead of remounting immediately, she walked Stella a few feet off the path so that she could soak it all in and breathe in the ocean air. The wind blowing in her ears muted the world around her. It was because of that wind that she was caught off guard when a rider on a black horse charged out of the forest on the path a few feet away, scaring Stella, who leaped to the left, almost knocking Sarah off her feet. She fought to hang onto the reins as Stella backed up and reared.

The rider on the black horse drew his horse to a stop and turned his horse around, but made no move to dismount and help.

"Whoa," she said to the mare in a low voice, calming her. Once she was reasonably assured Stella was okay and so was she, she turned to find the rider and his horse watching her.

"You all right?" he finally asked.

"No thanks to you," she barked at him, the adrenaline from the experience still coursing through her veins.

"Sorry about that. I didn't see you there at first."

"You probably ought to be more careful in the future and not go charging like a bat-out-of-hell on a narrow path like that. Especially with limited visibility." Her tone reminded her of her mother. The man smiled at her. "Noted." As her pulse regained a steady rhythm, she was able to see more clearly. For the first time she noticed him as more than an annoyance. He had dark hair and brown eyes, and he appeared to be mid-thirties. Attractive. Probably a wealthy playboy from one of those manor houses she saw high up on the hill before she entered the forest.

Now that she had Stella calmed down, she rechecked the girth and remounted.

"I am afraid we haven't met before," he said, watching her mount.

"And it's unlikely we'll meet again," she assured him, turning Stella back toward the forest path. But she didn't urge the mare forward. Instead, she stopped and looked at him. She didn't want to be a rude tourist and felt the need to at least smooth things over. "You don't have any wayward companions likely to charge me as I head back down the path do you?"

He shook his head. "Not that I'm aware of. You have to believe me, I am truly sorry. I didn't intend to frighten you or your horse."

His accent was different than some of the locals. Far more refined, and in some instances it seemed to disappear altogether. Yes, he definitely lived in a manor somewhere, she quickly decided.

"Very well. Apology accepted," she said, her tone matching his.

He urged the black gelding he rode alongside Stella. "I'm Kevin MacClery and this is Shadow."

"Sarah May and Stella." She gave him a polite smile and took the hand he offered, intending to give him a handshake.

But he lifted her hand to his lips and kissed the back of it instead.

Her heart fluttered for a second and she pulled her hand away once she felt he'd had hold of it for an appropriate amount of time.

"I just live a half mile east of here. Can I at least offer you a drink for your trouble? It's only a few minutes ride from here."

Immediate panic overwhelmed her. Not because she was afraid of him, but because of the physical reaction he'd caused. "This is a rented horse and I probably should get back."

"Vacation then?"

She nodded and forced a smile. "I'm here with friends."

"Where are you staying?"

He was certainly inquisitive. "Back in town," was all she said.

"So will you come have a drink with me?" he asked again. "I should get back, I don't want them to worry..." she started. She wasn't in the habit of running off with strange men she'd only just met.

"Is the horse from O'Leary's? I'm sure they won't mind if you stay out a bit longer. I'll call Lily to let her know the horse will be an hour later, and I'll even ride back with you." He flashed another brilliant smile at her.

He had incredibly straight teeth and through those teeth he was a smooth talker. Persistent too.

Drawing in a deep breath, Sarah relented, but only because curiosity got the best of her. She would love to get a look inside a big house like that, provided she was right and he lived in one of them. Besides, he didn't give off a bad vibe and she prided herself on being a pretty good judge of character. "All right, but only for a few minutes. I want to make sure Stella gets back by feeding time."

"I'll make sure it happens." He whirled his horse around and started forward. Ahead, the path forked. One path began winding down toward the ocean, the other went

left. He took the path going left and Sarah and Stella followed.

After a few hundred yards the path grew wider and Kevin turned back toward her. "You want to race?"

Before it even registered what he'd asked, Kevin and Shadow bolted off like a shot, at a full gallop ahead.

Sarah had never been that reckless so she urged Stella into a trot, then into a canter, following him.

He reached the house long before she did, but then she hadn't tried to catch up. Just as she suspected, the manor house was large and daunting, rising up from the flat hilltop a monstrosity overlooking the ocean from one side and the hills from the other.

The barn was off to the right of the house. Kevin dismounted and began unsaddling the black gelding. Two men emerged from the barn and rushed up to help him.

"We'll be going back out in an hour so she can get the mare back to O'Leary's," he was saying.

She stopped Stella beneath an oak tree and climbed off, carefully drawing the stirrups up the saddle. One of the men took Stella's reins from her. "I can do that, Miss."

"Let Frank do that," Kevin said, motioning her to follow him.

With a bit of hesitation, she left the mare with the man and followed Kevin toward the house.

"I usually take care of my horse myself, but since your time is limited, I thought it would give us more time to talk if we let my stable manager and his helper take care of them. I hope that's all right." He seemed overly concerned that she thought so.

She obliged. "Sure it's okay. Why wouldn't it be?"

"I suppose I wouldn't want you to think I'm a jerk. I'm

not helpless or spoiled." He motioned toward the lavish house.

"Well, that depends."

"On?"

"Whether you inherited your good fortune or made it yourself."

"Ah. Well then, I guess I'm sad to say that I did inherit the family business." He opened the door and stood aside so she could go in first.

"And what's the family business?"

"Shipping," he said. "Sounds boring." He nodded. "It is."

She went in ahead of him, wincing when she realized her boots were dirty and she would likely spread dirt and mud on the rugs and marble floors. Stopping where she was, she decided not to step off the rug. "Should I take off my boots?"

"That might be best. Beth might kill us both if she finds mud and dirt tracked through the house." He took off his boots revealing plain black socks underneath.

Sarah felt a bit more comfortable then, and removed her paddock boots, grateful she had decided against bringing her field boots, which were harder to get in and out of without a boot jack.

Now both in stocking feet, Kevin led her through a grand sitting room, through a formal dining room, and into a modern kitchen with a bay windowed breakfast nook looking out over the forest and the fern colored hills below. She immediately went over to inspect the scenery.

"So we should have that drink, then? What will you have?" He put some ice in a bowl and started back toward the sitting room.

She followed him, contemplating if she just enjoyed hearing his regal accent or if it was the way he carried himself. A pang of guilt hit her in the gut. How could she be thinking this with her fiancé only dead five months? *It wasn't right*, she warned herself.

"Actually, just water would be fine," she said, quickly deciding that she better not drink.

"I can make you a Manhattan," he suggested, not acknowledging her water comment.

"I shouldn't drink and ride." With a forced smiled she turned away from him, pretending to be interested in some of the photographs on the mantel. There, pictures of Kevin and a beautiful woman looked back at him. His girlfriend? Or worse, his wife? Maybe a sister. "Your family?"

He stopped what he was doing and went over to her to see which picture she was looking at. "That's my late wife, Gabriella."

"Oh, I'm sorry…" she felt another pang of guilt, but this time for possibly bringing up something sad.

"No, don't be. She's been gone seven years now, but I haven't the heart to put the pictures away yet."

What were the odds?

"How about you? Do you have someone back the U.S.?" He went back to the bar and started working on the drinks again, measuring, mixing, shaking.

"My fiancé…" she paused, noticing how listless her voice sounded, "He was killed in Iraq five months ago."

Kevin stopped what he was doing and leaned on the bar. "Oh. Sorry for your loss. I didn't mean to bring it up…"

"No, it's all right." Sarah drew in a deep breath and forced a smile. She remembered back to the night before they left for Ireland and how she'd put Eric's photograph away. "I couldn't bring myself to keep the photograph on the mantel. I decided to pack everything up and sell the house."

Kevin's eyes searched her face. "Gabriella had brain

cancer. We knew a year before she died that she was dying."

Sarah looked at the vibrant, beautiful blonde in the picture. "She was so young."

"A wise man once said none of us is guaranteed another day," he said. Then he finished making the drinks and handed her a filled martini glass. "I promise you'll like it."

Then he lifted his glass. "*Sláinte*, or perhaps *Carpe Diem* is more appropriate."

She lifted her glass in response then took a sip of the drink. It wasn't half bad. A deep sigh escaped her lips. Then she asked him the question she needed the answer to, "How long does the pain last?"

His dark eyes searched the depth of his glass, then those soulful eyes lifted to meet hers. "You know how people say time heals all wounds?"

"I've heard that."

"Well, that's not true." He swirled the alcohol around in his glass. "Time makes the pain more bearable. That's all. It took me a while to realize that Gabriella wouldn't want me moping around the house, shutting myself off from the world. She'd have wanted me to move on and be happy. To live my life. I imagine your fiancé would have wanted the same thing."

"Eric," she said. "His name was Eric."

Kevin lifted his glass again. "To Eric and Gabriella, may they both rest in peace."

Sarah could drink to that, so she did, and drained the rest of the glass. Though she'd never been a drinker, she wanted another one, and Kevin obliged.

"So what made you decide to come to Ireland for a vacation?"

She shrugged and smiled. "My friends. They've been worried about me, especially Kate. I think she thinks I'm going to try to harm myself or something."

His tone turned suddenly serious. "You don't feel the urge to hurt yourself, do you?"

"God no. Of course I do admit I've been depressed, but that's normal, right?"

"Understandably so," he said. "How about I get us some lunch."

In agreement, she followed him into the kitchen.

Two hours, some tears, some laughter, shared stories about vacations with Gabriella and Eric, some soda bread, cheese, pear chutney, and one alcoholic beverage later, Sarah realized the time. "Oh crap, it's late."

He looked at the grandfather clock in the corner of the room. "It seems I've kept you longer than I should have and I forgot to call the stable to let them know you still had the horse. Let me do that now."

She hurried to the door and put her boots back on, not feeling the alcohol in the least. The entire experience talking to Kevin had been cathartic. Perhaps it was because he was a complete stranger, or maybe it was because he'd been through the loss of someone he loved, too. Either way, she wasn't sorry she'd come, she was only sorry that the light was fading fast outside. She could hear his voice in the other room talking to someone. He returned straight away.

"Good news, the stable hasn't sent out a search party yet. They just figured you lost track of time, but they were getting ready to send someone. Evidently one of your friends called to see if you were back yet. How about we both ride down and I have one of my guys meet us with the car and we can drive you back to your hotel?"

"Cottage," she corrected.

With a nod of acknowledgment, he put on his boots and together they went back out to the stable to find Stella was re- saddled. One of Kevin's men agreed to meet them at the stable. Kevin climbed into the saddle first, helping Sarah climb up behind him. She put her hands around his waist and breathed in his spicy scent. How she missed the closeness of a male body.

The ride back didn't take as long as the ride there had.

There were periods of comfortable silence and Sarah fought the urge to rest her cheek on Kevin's back. Instead, she kept a polite distance and only hung on with a light touch around his waist. Once or twice his strong hand came down over hers as if he was checking to make sure she was still holding on.

About half way down to the stable Kevin finally spoke up. "This region has a lot of small historical sites you can only get to by horseback. A few miles out there's an old wedge tomb. If you're interested in experiencing some Irish history, I could come get you, and you and I could ride out there tomorrow afternoon and take lunch with us. I have a horse you can ride."

"Okay," she agreed with a smile. It sounded fun and there was no harm in it. By the time they reached the stable and the nervous teenage stable hand who seemed relieved to see the horse was still alive, Sarah was pretty sure Kevin MacClery's friendship, even if it was just for the duration of her vacation, was exactly what she needed. Someone who knew what she was going through. Someone who wouldn't judge her or worry about her needlessly. And if he kissed her, even though she expected no such thing, she'd already decided she would let him.

7

The Beach

It seemed odd they would all head out in different directions the second day there, but Sarah wanted to go horseback riding and neither Em nor Kate saw any reason to stop her. Kate had decided to scout the town for great food and shopping since for her this was, in part, a working vacation. It made her trip a tax write off, as she told her friends. Emily, on the other hand, just wanted to hang out and see the scenery. It was a two-mile walk to the beach, but she didn't mind. Since she wasn't getting any gym time, she figured a little exercise would be good for her. Besides, driving or taking a taxi didn't allow for the kind of reflection time and sightseeing that Emily liked. She didn't want to be rushed and walking seemed the best way to experience the Irish countryside in one of the most comfortable ways possible.

When she made it to the shore, she found herself surprised at how much it looked like some of the parts of the East Coast she'd been to. Of course, this was just the other side of the Atlantic. She wasn't sure if she expected something softer, like the beaches of Southern California or the Bahamas. She laughed. Of course not, she told herself. It seemed anywhere it could get cold in winter, craggy, rocky beaches were eminent. It was beautiful nonetheless. She breathed in the salty air and closed her eyes. She'd seen a few other people walking. An older man had even tipped his head at her in polite acknowledgment. She was thankful for the light jacket she brought because the breeze over the cold Atlantic sent goose pimples across the smooth skin of her arms. Drawing the jacket around her, she hugged her arms close to her chest.

She took out her phone and took a few pictures to send to Lucy and Mom. They were already raving, via text, how awesome yesterday's pictures of the cottage hillside looked. Lucy, of course, was upset that Em hadn't brought her along. Perhaps someday she'd come back and bring both Mom and Lucy with her. It wasn't a strange idea at all. That would surely upset Sam and he'd have to one-up her by dragging Lucy to the French Riviera or something. Lucy wouldn't mind, of course, but Emily would. She never wanted Lucy to end up as a weapon used between them, but every time she turned around, it seemed that's what Sam did. He had to one-up her no matter what she did, and most of what she did was not done to make Sam look bad. He just took it that way. She'd bought Lucy an iPad for school because it was on the school supply list. Sam, looking for his father-of-the-year award, turned around and bought her a new iPhone and a MacBook. Innocent stuff like that. If she bought Lucy school clothes, Cheri would take Lucy for a girl's day to buy an expensive outfit that no rational parent would buy for a twelve-year-old who would likely grow out of it in six months' time. While Lucy saw right through Cheri's spa days and shopping sprees, she enjoyed them and the bragging rights they earned. Her friends were surely in awe of her Prada bag. *Who gives a Prada bag to a twelve-year-old?* Seriously. She let out a sigh and took in another deep breath. This walk was just what she needed.

With a glance at her watch, she decided to start heading back and maybe she'd walk to the pub for lunch and see if Kate wanted to meet her. There was no reason to rush.

The walk back seemed to go faster than the walk down to the ocean side, and she was able to find her way back to the road their cottage was on easily. She found herself breathing a bit harder. The walk down had been all downhill and she hadn't considered the fact that eventually she'd have to go back up. By the time she reached the O'Flannigan house her t- shirt was moist with perspiration. An older woman, perhaps in her mid to late fifties, stood sweeping the porch.

Emily smiled sweetly and said, "Hi."

"You one of the young women staying at the cottage?"

"Yes, Ma'am," Em said, wanting to be as polite as possible.

"Nice day for a walk then," the woman stated. She kept pulling the broom across the lacquered slats of the porch, sweeping away imaginary dust. Or if it was dusty, Emily couldn't tell. It looked clean to her.

"It was. I went down to the beach and back. Now I want to change and go into town for lunch." She forced a smile even though she wanted to end this conversation and hurry back to the cottage for a quick shower and a change of clothes. Of course she would have to walk back into town for lunch. This is where splitting up and only having one car between the three of them was a bit of a chore.

"You'll be needing a ride then," the woman said without skipping a beat. She seemed to notice Emily was sweating. "Otherwise, you'll need to change again. I'll send Sean over to fetch you and take you into town. About a half an hour?"

"Oh, no, really, it's okay..." she stammered, more concerned about having to get a ride with a strange man rather than whether or not she'd have to walk and take a shower for a third time today.

"Nonsense. It's no trouble. He'll be around in a half an hour. Go on then." The woman nodded toward the cottage and smiled.

By the look on the woman's face, Em knew it was settled and it would be no use arguing. Instead, she graciously surrendered, swallowing her pride. "Thanks. I appreciate it."

"It's no trouble at all dear," the woman repeated and went back to sweeping the imaginary dust from the front porch.

Emily made her way back to the cottage. Deep down, she'd hoped she would get there and find Kate had come back for something, but if she knew anything about Kate - Kate liked to be where the action was. It was doubtful Kate would spend much time at the cottage at all unless Sarah and Emily were with her. No, she'd stay in town where she could mingle with the locals and get the scoop on the local cuisine and nightlife, and then in the evening hours, she'd drag Em and Sarah with her unless one of them vehemently protested. At least Sarah wouldn't abandon Emily. The only reason they weren't together now is that Sarah wanted to go horseback riding and Emily didn't ride. There was no sense on Sarah missing out on a potential once-in-a-lifetime chance, so Emily didn't protest. Besides, she was glad she'd taken the walk.

Inside, she hurried and jumped in the shower for a quick rinse, then changed into jeans and a solid blue t-shirt with a sensible pair of walking flats. There was no reason to dress up. Besides, they were on vacation. Who wanted to wear uncomfortable clothes and shoes while relaxing in a foreign country?

She grabbed her handbag from the bedside table and made sure her wallet and passport were tucked neatly inside, then she went out in front of the cottage to wait. A quick text to Kate asked where she was.

"At a shop," came the response.

"Lunch at Pub?" Emily typed, then added: "I've got a ride."

"K, see U in a few," Kate typed back.

After waiting ten minutes, Emily started up the road. She wasn't going to wait for Sean O'Flannigan to pick her up. It was just like a man to be both unreliable and late. But just as she reached the crest of the hill, his pickup, a single-cab white Toyota Hilux, the bed filled with straw bales, came over it. Both the driver and passenger side windows were down. He stopped beside her. "It seems I'm your ride into town."

Emily fought back the urge to say *'No thank you'* and instead smiled politely. "Only if it's no trouble. Otherwise, I can walk."

"No trouble at all," he said. His voice only hinted at the lilting Irish accent his mother had. His eyes looked her up and down and he motioned to the passenger side. "Climb in."

Once she was safely inside, he turned the truck around in the cottage drive, and they started back toward town.

"You don't have much of an accent," she said, not caring if the statement seemed rude.

"I went to school in the United States. Williams College." He kept his gray eyes on the road. "I taught myself how to speak without as much of an accent."

Some conversation was better than awkward silence and the fact that he'd been to the States piqued her curiosity. "Oh? What did you study?"

"Biochemistry and molecular biology." He glanced at her to gauge her reaction. "Of course, when my father died I had a choice. I could move my mother into a flat, sell the farm, and move to wherever I could find a good job in a laboratory, or I could come home, take care of my mother, and run the farm."

She tried not to act surprised, but she was. Mostly because she'd judged him to be some loser living with his mom because he didn't have a choice. *A lesson in judging people by their looks learned,* she said to herself, knowing full well she'd likely do it again at some point in the future, even though she would tell herself she didn't mean to. "I can't imagine having to make that kind of decision. But if it helps, I live with my mom, too."

"She needs help?"

Emily shook her head and decided she should come clean as penance for being judgmental. "No. My daughter and I moved back home after the divorce."

The truth was Emily didn't have to live with her mother. She wanted to. There was something comforting and stabilizing about living with her mom that made the divorce not-so-bad. Sure, she could tell herself all day long that her mother needed help, but the truth was her mom was only in her late fifties and spry as could be. She still worked, but as a novelist and magazine writer, she worked from home. That's why she didn't mind watching after Lucy as much as she did. Even if Em had moved herself and Lucy into an apartment or townhouse somewhere, her mom still would have watched Lucy after school and during the summer while Emily worked. There was a span of uncomfortable silence between them.

Finally, Sean said, "Well, I'm sure she enjoys having you and your daughter there with her."

That was probably true. Her mom couldn't give up the house after Emily's dad passed away. She said it was too much a part of her life and she wanted to stay in her house as long as she could. It was a big house and likely lonely without Lucy and Emily there. Perhaps that's why her mom hadn't protested when they moved in and seemed happy as a lark to have them there with her. "Yeah, I think she does. The house is big and she didn't want to sell it."

Sean kept his eyes on the road. "Family is important."

She couldn't hold back the snort, or the snarky comment. "Too bad my ex-didn't think that way, or we'd still be married."

Then she cringed and frowned at her bad manners. "Sorry. I'm trying not to be hateful and bitter, or to drag strangers into my problems. It was highly inappropriate for me to say that."

"It's better to get the anger out than hold it in," he said simply, a small smile playing on his lips.

"So, anyplace we must absolutely try for dinner while we're here?" she asked, trying to change the subject to something lighter. Though it was likely Kate had already asked this question.

"The restaurant attached to the pub is very good. My friend Aedan cooks for both," he said, matter-of-factly. "Dinner at the pub last night wasn't half bad either. That's why I'm going back for lunch today," she said. Looking out at the sky she was surprised how clear it was. Everything she'd read suggested rain was common on your average spring afternoon in Ireland. "I bet Sarah is enjoying her ride."

"Your other friend?" Sean asked.

Emily nodded. "She loves horseback riding, but Kate and I don't ride, so she went alone."

"Lots of trails for that around here," he said, easing into boring small talk. She thought she detected a slight hint of disappointment in his voice.

She looked over at him, realizing how attractive he was. Not just his physical appearance. Years of farm work had certainly kept his upper body strong and she bet he had a six pack under that shirt, but he was also smart if he had a degree in biochemistry and molecular biology, and she found intelligence highly attractive.

He caught her looking.

Her eyes quickly diverted back to the road. This car trip seemed to be taking longer than she expected.

"So do you and your friends plan on doing any sightseeing while you're here?"

"I think so," she said. Though she wasn't sure Kate was the sight-seeing type. Kate wanted to interact with people, not places. "At least Sarah and I plan on it. We might just take the car and leave Kate off wherever she wants to explore." She felt the need to explain when he gave her a questioning look. "Kate is all about people and food.

Nightlife. Sarah and I are more your low-key, sight-seeing tourists."

He chuckled. "Ah. Well if you need any suggestions for local sights, let me know. I know of a castle not far from here that is open to the public for tours."

"Thank you. I think we'd love to know how to get there. I'll check with Sarah." She gave him a broad smile and realized he had pulled up right outside the pub.

"Here you are."

"Thanks so much. You saved me a long walk." A little disappointed the ride was over, she got out. She thought about asking him in to eat with them, but quickly decided against it. "Have a great afternoon."

"You too..." he paused as if waiting for something. "Emily," she told him, realizing in horror and embarrassment she hadn't even shared her name. "And you're Sean..."

A slow smile spread over his lips and he nodded. "That's right. I'll see you later Emily. Have a nice lunch."

She gave him a nod, feeling the heat in her cheeks, and then slowly turned toward the building and went inside. It wasn't until she was in the cool dark pub that smelled of oiled wood and beer that she turned around to see Sean and his truck disappear down the road.

"You hitched a ride from Sean?"

Kate's voice from behind her caused her to jump. "Yeah, he was kind enough to give me a lift."

"Where's Sarah?"

"Still riding I imagine," Emily said absently as she tried to regain her composure. "Where should we sit?"

"At the bar?"

Emily frowned. "Nah, table over there."

She pointed to a table in the corner. Kate shrugged and went to the table, climbing into a chair. "You and Sarah can be so anti-social."

"No, we just enjoy our alone time. It recharges us.

We're introverts. That's why we keep you around," she said and winked at Kate, who laughed.

A barman stopped by the table. "What'll you have?"

"A Guinness and a bowl of Irish stew, please," said Emily. "Could I get some bread with that, too? And a salad?"

The man nodded then looked at Kate, who gave Emily a strange look. "I'll do the same."

Once the man was gone with their order, Kate leaned across the table to Emily. "What's up with you? You seem a bit... I don't know how to describe it."

Emily shook her head. "Nothing," she lied. "I'm just a bit tired from that long walk I took earlier. Perhaps after lunch you could drop me off at the cottage so I could have a nap before dinner?"

"A nap?" Kate appeared disappointed. "I thought we would do some shopping."

She gave Em a hopeful smile.

With a sigh, Emily relented. "Okay. Shopping, then dinner, but I need my beauty sleep. Sean says there's a castle we can tour not far from here. Maybe we'll do that tomorrow."

A sly smile slid across Kate's lips. "Sean?"

"What?"

"Not Mr. O'Flannigan?" Kate's grin grew bigger until it had reached Cheshire cat proportions. "I thought you thought he was a serial killer?"

"Oh shut up." She shook her head.

Just then the barman set two glasses of water in front of them along with their stew, salads, and bread. "The beer's still pourin' ladies. I'll have it out to you in a bit."

"We certainly don't want to rush the pour," Kate said with a smile. "Thank you."

The man reacted how all men reacted to Kate's flirty demeanor, with a gallant smile and a swagger to his step. Emily shook her head. "What?"

"You're such a flirt."

"Yeah, but we get better service - admit it." Kate lifted her water to her lips and drank, and then she appraised her stew. "*Bon appetit!*"

With a quick smile, Kate picked up her spoon, dug into the Irish stew and put a spoonful in her mouth, only to wretch it up onto her empty bread plate with a complete look of disgust on her face.

Panic rose in Emily's gut. "What's wrong?"

"Don't eat that, it's gross." Kate pushed the spoon through the contents of the plate to find the offending morsel. "This…"

She held up a piece of what appeared to be, an artery, then dropped it back on the plate. Lifting a hand to summon the barman she said, "Excuse me. Could I speak to the chef?"

Emily wanted to crawl under the table because all eyes in the pub were on them and she knew Kate wasn't going to let it go. Even though Kate was relatively friendly and easy-going personally, professionally she was like the female version of Gordon Ramsay, only as a food critic instead of a master chef.

8

Local Wanderer

"What's wrong?" the barman asked.

"There are animal arteries in this stew. I'd like to know if he paid attention to the meat cuts he put into this stew. I hear your chef is allegedly one of the best in the county. My review may not reflect that." Kate's demeanor had gone cold and her voice carried through the pub, summoning people from the kitchen. She had no intention of letting it go. When she paid for a meal, it was, at least, edible. Sure, it may not have received a favorable review, but edible was all she ever asked.

"What's all this noise then?" said a tall, attractive blond from the door of the kitchen.

"Aedan, this lady wants to talk to you about your stew." The barman looked at Kate and motioned toward the blond man, who looked Swedish more than Irish, and said,

"There you are. He's the chef."

Aedan came over to the table, glanced at Emily who was looking down, and looked at Kate, who pointed down at the artery. "Animal artery. You realize how disgusting that is for someone to find in their stew? It's even more dangerous for a food critic to find one in her stew."

"You're a food critic huh? Let me guess, you have a blog? Or do you write for some offbeat local paper back home?" It was clear at this point that Aedan wasn't going to bow to her food critic status like most chefs did. Instead he manipulated the situation to where he had the upper hand.

"You're changing the subject," Kate said in a curt voice, trying to get control back. "Why is there an animal artery in the stew?"

"I don't know. It probably made it in there by mistake. Such things sometimes happen." Half his mouth upturned into a smile making it obvious he was trying hard not to laugh.

"Well, my friend and I aren't eating the stew."

"I can see how an artery could make you go off it," he said, completely taking away any hope she had of getting the upper hand back. He turned to the barman, "Let's take away the bowls."

Then he turned back to both women. "Are the salads and bread satisfactory?"

Kate couldn't help but feel he was being condescending. "They're fine. It's kind of hard to screw up salad and bread. Perhaps you could make something else we could try? Provided you're able to cook it adequately and the ingredients aren't *scraps*."

The man's green eyes went wide and he gave her a look that suggested he might say something else, but he held back. "I can make you some nice bangers and mash."

"What do you want, Em?" Kate said, wondering what the chef was thinking.

"Perhaps some nice boxty? Shepherd's pie? Pasties? Or maybe some Coddle?" He kept throwing menu items out. "Bacon and cabbage?"

Emily looked up at the chef apologetically. "I'll just have boxty, please."

"And I'll try the Dublin coddle so long as it doesn't have cow arteries floating around in it," Kate said, flashing him a disingenuous smile.

Em's hands went to her face.

The chef nodded. "Very well then. We'll try again."

With that, he turned on his heel and went back into the kitchen, not looking back even once.

"Why'd you only get the boxty? You know that's just potato pancakes, right?" Kate didn't get Emily sometimes. She would have been the type to take the cow artery out of her mouth, set it aside, and politely eat the rest of the stew. But Kate knew better. When restaurants had a bad dish, it was best to call them on it.

Emily shook her head. "So I can see the spit on it." With a laugh, Kate leaned in. "He wouldn't dare."

"You were a complete bitch to the guy. I'm sure the artery in the stew was a mistake," Emily assured her. "Whatever. He sure acts high on himself. Most chefs are like that though, and did you hear what he asked me? He thought I was a blogger." She paused when the barman brought them their glasses of Guinness, but picked up before he left. "Usually all I have to do is tell people I'm Kate Berkhill from Food and Travel Dining magazine."

The barman hurried off and disappeared back in the kitchen.

Kate laughed. "Did you see that?"

"This isn't funny. We're either going to be banned from the local pub, or you're getting something nasty put in your food, our food, if you keep it up," Emily said in a warning tone. "Besides, can't you give the guy a break? Did you know he's a friend of Sean O'Flannigan?"

Her face fell and she stopped her gloating. "Okay, I see your point."

"Yeah, the last thing we need to do is piss off the landlord and the local pub people in one shot," Emily said with a shrug.

"Fair enough." Kate didn't have an argument for that because Emily was right. It probably wasn't wise to burn too many bridges. They still had two weeks and five days to go and if they had to eat in the neighboring town the rest of the trip, it might get tedious since it was a further drive by about fifteen to twenty minutes.

"So what's a Dublin Coddle?" Em asked, trying to ease any tension.

"It's a hot pot. Usually with sausage, potato, bacon and onions.

It's likely safe. You can try some of mine," Kate offered.

With a wary look, Emily shook her head and poked at her salad. "I'll try it on another visit, if we ever come back here."

It took another ten minutes, but this time, Aedan brought their lunch out to them personally, then pulled up a chair and sat down, crossing his arms over his chest. "Go on then, try it. I'll wait right here while you grade me," he said to Kate.

He winked at Emily.

As Emily fought back a laugh at Kate's expense, Kate picked up her fork and speared a sausage, a potato with bacon pieces on it, and a slice of onion, then put them in her mouth. It was hot, but not hot enough to burn her tongue. The fried bacon added a lot of flavor to the potatoes, and the onions were slightly sweet. The sausage was savory and complemented the potatoes nicely. Taking her time chewing and swallowing, she weighed her choice of words carefully. "Thank you, this is better."

She shifted the pieces of meat and vegetable around, looking for anything he might have hidden.

"Don't worry, you won't find any surprises," he said. "Now, are you all good here?"

"Yes, thank you and we're sorry if it was any inconvenience..." Emily started.

Kate interrupted. "This is better, thank you."

He shook his head, went to the bar and took a seat. He glanced over in their direction a few times.

Emily returned a stern look. "Three weeks left. Sean's friend."

With a groan, Kate rolled her eyes like a despondent teenager. Then with a sigh she lifted an eyebrow at Emily. "We really need to work on that passive aggressive peace-keeping thing you've got going on."

While she didn't want to say anything to hurt Emily's feelings, there was a reason Emily had stayed with a man who was verbally abusive for so long. It's because she preferred to keep the peace and not rock the boat.

Obviously that stance hadn't gotten her far in relationships. To be honest, Kate was surprised Emily had such a good job, since she rarely ever stood up for herself or took charge. At least not to people's faces. The only people Emily was ever herself around were Kate and Sarah. Or at least, that's all Kate had ever seen.

Emily didn't respond to Kate's comment, instead she went at her potato pancakes with vigor. "These are very good."

"Let me try." She reached over and took a piece of the boxty and put it in her mouth. By far, that was the best potato pancake she'd ever tasted. It was even better than some of the Eastern European potato pancakes she'd had. "I'll give the potato pancake four stars."

"That's easily five stars and you know it," Emily said, shaking her head.

"They lose a point because they weren't accompanied by groveling." Kate threw on an evil grin and took another bite of hot pot.

Em sighed and shook her head again. "You're a

horrible little person, Kate Berkhill. If you don't change your ways, you're going to die old and alone."

"How do you figure?"

"As I see it, you're taking out your frustration with Josh and your sister on that poor chef."

Well, that was blunt. Kate held back a *harrumph*. "Just like you're projecting your bitterness at Sam on all males?"

"Yes. The difference is my *mistrust* of men is due to years of psychological abuse and conditioning from a bad relationship. Whereas you're just being sadistic and enjoying hurting others to bury your own hurt." Emily smiled sweetly.

"Fine, I'll drop it and I'll give him five stars on the boxty, and four on the hot pot," she conceded, not realizing he'd come up alongside the table.

"I'll take four stars on the hot pot and the boxty was my grandmother's recipe so I can't take credit for the five stars there," said Aedan with a half-grin. "Can I get you ladies anything else?"

Despite her irritation, she decided to be pleasant. Not with Emily pointing out a possible truth, and the fact that Aedan had been nice and accommodating.

"Since I'm being graded," he said, pulling up a chair. "Perhaps I can at least know your name?"

Now she was suspicious. Was he trying to get on her good side? Her eyes narrowed. "You first."

Emily's jaw dropped and she shook her head.

With a sigh, Aedan sat back. "I'm Aedan O'Byrne. You already know I'm the chef at this establishment."

"So you don't own this place Aedan O'Byrne?" Kate asked, trying not to sound rude. It wasn't working.

"No. I just work here, but the man who owns it will be

pleased if we were included favorably in an article." He smiled.

"Her name is Kate Berkhill and she's not usually this bitchy," said Emily from across the table. "I'm Emily Frost, Kate's rather embarrassed friend."

Kate looked at the empty beer glass in front of Emily and winced. Emily didn't hold her liquor well. It definitely lowered her inhibitions, and since Emily's strongest inhibition was being open and up front with people, she naturally turned into an honest extrovert when she drank.

Aedan shook Emily's offered hand with an amused look on his face. "It's a pleasure to make your acquaintance. Can I get you another Guinness, Emily?"

"I don't think that's a wise idea," Kate jumped in. "Em doesn't usually drink."

"I drank that beer on a full stomach," Emily protested. "Yes, please, I'll have another."

He lifted Emily's empty glass and nodded at the bartender, who nodded back. Aedan turned his attention back to Kate. "So, Kate Berkhill, I take it you enjoy checking out local eateries. This must be a working trip for you."

He didn't wait for an answer.

"I can give you a list. There are a lot of great places within twenty-five miles of here. Enough for several articles worth. If you'd like recommendations, that is." His green eyes bore into her expectantly.

Before Kate could answer, Emily blurted, "Of course she would. I bet she'd also like a tour of your *kitchen*."

A flush of crimson crept into Kate's cheeks. "No, she shouldn't have any more beer."

He laughed. "She'll be fine. Besides, I'd love to show you my kitchen."

She wanted to narrow her eyes in suspicion but she held back. She'd had chefs kiss up to her, but this was ridiculous, and Emily's commentary wasn't helping.

Instead, she forced a polite smile and went into business mode, the side of herself she reserved for her editors. "Well then yes, I'd like to see it."

With a warning glance in Emily's direction, she followed Aedan back into the kitchen. Emily gave her a broad smile as the barman set a second pint of Guinness in front of her.

Good God she was going to have to either take Emily home after this or wait until she sobered up if they still wanted to go shopping. She considered texting Sarah to get reinforcements, but quickly decided against it. If anyone deserved a day riding horses across the Irish countryside unfettered by worry for her friends, it was Sarah. This vacation was primarily all about helping her, after all.

Shoving everything to the back of her mind, she followed Aedan into the pristine, white and stainless steel kitchen. It was immaculate. Off to the side sat a table.

"Chef's table?" she asked, surprised.

"Yes, from the restaurant side. Believe it or not, our restaurant is a frequent stop for politicians and more affluent travelers on their way from the north to Dublin." His tone wasn't arrogant at all, just proud of his accomplishment. It was no small feat to turn a quaint pub and restaurant in a modest town into something worthy of the rich and famous.

"Impressive. Everything is so clean..." She wasn't sure she'd ever seen a kitchen so spotless.

"I can't work in a cluttered or dirty kitchen. Brian and Robert, my assistants, this is Miss Kate Berkhill. She's a food critic," he said.

The one called Brian smirked. "Aren't they all?"

"No, she's a proper food critic," Aedan said in a warning tone.

Brian shook his head and went back to washing down one of the grill surfaces.

"Do I get to inspect the freezer?" Kate asked, turning back into her fun-loving flirty self.

Aedan turned to her, tipped his head slightly and bit his lower lip. "Do you want to look in the freezer? I was thinking we could visit the wine storage."

That perked her right up. "Wine storage?"

"It's not quite a cellar, so we don't call it a wine cellar. But it is dark and kept at thirteen degrees Celsius. We're quite proud of it." He kept leading her, past the freezers and bread racks with fresh bread.

In her head she tried to do the math to convert Celsius to Fahrenheit. Why did Americans insist on being so different from the rest of the civilized world? "That's a…"

"Fifty-five Fahrenheit," he offered as if he could read her mind.

"Conversion is a tricky thing." She threw him a chagrined smile.

He typed in a code on a keypad backlit with a green glow, and stepped into the wine room, motioning her inside. Behind them, the door closed. "Here we are. We just put it in last month. My pride and joy. We have quite the collection, too. Some wonderful imported French wines, including a 1995 *Château Rayas.*"

She was impressed. "That's a pricey bottle of wine. I can see why you keep the door locked."

"Over seven-hundred-twenty-nine euros a bottle." He paused as if thinking what to say. "That's about eight-hundred American dollars."

"How do you do those conversions so quickly in your head?" She followed him out of the wine room.

He locked the door when they were out. "I've always been good with maths."

She smiled at his more appropriate English. "You find that amusing?"

"Not exactly. I find your use of the word *maths* as opposed to just *math* interesting. The differences between British English and American English are fascinating to me." She winced a little, hoping she didn't offend him.

"Well, you say mathematics, yes? You would never say mathematic," he reasoned. "Therefore, maths is more appropriate than math."

"Well reasoned indeed," she said. He did have a point. She would have never guessed she'd meet an Irish chef who was also a grammar maven and good with maths. With a deep breath, she looked back toward the pub entrance to the kitchen. "Well thank you for the tour but I should get back to Emily. I might need to sober her up before I decide what else my afternoon has in store."

"You should come to dinner tonight. Here. Be guests at my table? I'll make you and your friends a four-course dinner. Tonight I'm serving tomato and basil salad or feta cheese mousse, cured and smoked duck breast, or you can have the cured salmon, and loin of rabbit, or sea bass, finished off with your choice of a cheese plate or a coffee and vanilla parfait. Each course with complementary wine, of course." He gave her a hopeful look.

Now he was talking. A rush of excitement coursed through her chest. This would be perfect - a review of *Mulligan's*, but she'd have to make sure Sarah and Emily were both on board. "Let me talk to my friends, but I'm sure we can come."

"Well, the table is now reserved for you. About seven?" He winked at her.

She felt herself blush. "Thank you. I should…go…"

"I know," he said. "Emily is waiting. Have a lovely afternoon Kate Berkhill. I look forward to cooking for you tonight."

Walking toward the door and looking over her shoulder, she almost ran into one of the assistants coming from the pub. She apologized and hurried back into the darkness of the pub and Emily, who was sitting at the table across from a tall man. When Kate's eyes adjusted to the light, she realized it was Sean O'Flannigan.

9

Finding Sarah

When Sean O'Flannigan stepped into the pub, Emily didn't see him. It wasn't until he took the chair right across from her that she noticed him at all.

"We meet again," he said. In his hand, he held what looked like a few brochures. He set them down and pushed them across the table to her. "The castle I was telling you about. I thought you might like better information."

The smile she gave him was almost reflexive and caused her cheeks to flush like a school-girl. "Thank you."

"Have you had lunch?"

Maybe it was the beer gone to her head, but she felt slightly flustered. "Oh, yes, but I'm just waiting for Kate. She's in the kitchen. With Aedan. I mean…"

Sean laughed. "That's Aedan."

"No, see, she's a food critic and he offered to give her a tour of the kitchen," she explained, feeling like a complete idiot. Maybe she shouldn't have had the second beer. Kate was right, Emily didn't hold her liquor well. *Calm yourself*, she scolded inwardly.

"It seems you and your friends all have different priorities for your vacation," he observed, looking toward the kitchen, then back at her. "If for any reason you find yourself at a loss for company to the castle, let me know."

Emily swallowed - hard. "Oh, thank you."

As if on cue, an equally flustered Kate stepped out of the kitchen and stopped dead, seeing Sean sitting at the table. A feeling of relief flooded Emily.

She grabbed her purse and the brochures and got up. "I suppose Kate and I should get going if we want to do some shopping."

Then she noticed Kate's purse still on the chair that Sean was sitting in.

Kate threw on a big smile and approached the table, not shy about grabbing her purse from behind Sean. "How are you, Mr. O'Flannigan?"

"Please, call me Sean. I was just telling Emily that if you and your other friend didn't want to go to the castle tomorrow I'd happily take her there myself," Sean smiled over at Em, then at Kate.

Kate gave Emily her *oh really?* look and smiled. Her eyebrows lifted when she said, "Oh, I see."

"Yeah, well, I'll let you know, but I'm pretty sure it will be a girls' day out," she said, taking Kate by the hand and pulling her along. "Thanks so much for everything, Sean."

She didn't stop until they were out on the sidewalk, almost a half block away from the pub.

"So what was up with that?" Kate asked.

"I don't know. I think I had too much to drink. My heart was in my stomach." She shrugged and took a deep breath. "So where to, shopping?"

Kate didn't say anything at first. But after a moment, she finally focused on the task at hand. "Let's go up to the shops this way."

Emily knew Kate wasn't finished though. Kate just hadn't formulated the right questions yet.

She followed her slender food critic friend to the first shop and they browsed.

"I think Sean is totally into you," she finally said. "You think so?" Em wasn't convinced. After all, she'd

only met the guy a few hours ago. "I think he's just being nice. I hear a lot of these small towns work on an old boys club, where they recommend their buddies shops, restaurants and sightseeing tours so all their friends profit."

"Oh, that's true," Kate agreed. "But if I know nothing else, I know when a guy is interested. Sean is a nice guy in general, I agree, but he's interested in you beyond just wanting to deliver you to his buddy's castle tour. Though I think both Sarah and I would like to do that, so he'll have to find another reason to get you alone."

"Ridiculous," Emily scoffed, feeling fear in the pit of her stomach. What if Kate was right? What if Sean *was* interested? Then what? She'd been officially divorced for six months now, but that was no reason to go leaping into some vacation romance with the first man who showed interest.

"No, it isn't. You're pretty hot," Kate assured her.

Emily laughed out loud. "Yeah, now I know you're pulling my leg."

"Ugh! Get Sam out of your head and say out loud, right now, *I am good looking, and there's a hot guy after my bod.*" Kate gave her a girlish smile.

"I will say no such thing. That's ridiculous." She shook her head. "I am not going to go all ga-ga over the first guy who flirts with me."

"He's not the first. Remember the night I took you to the *Octane Ice House*? There were like three guys hitting on you, but that cool attitude you gave them threw them off," Kate reminded her, her tone turning sober as she flipped through a rack of cashmere sweaters.

Emily did remember that night. She didn't remember guys hitting on her, but she did remember several rude men. "You mean the one guy who was trying to buy me drinks because he thought I was a cheap lay?"

"You're so cynical. He may have been trying to take you home, but it's because he thought you were good looking. He wasn't an ugly guy, Em. He was hot even by *my* standards. I could see you saying that if he was hideous or had a limp or something." Kate floated from rack to rack, browsing like a professional window shopper.

She had a point. If anything, Kate did tend to go for men who were attractive and knew it. If she thought a guy was good looking, he probably was, but he was probably a jerk, too. "So do you find Sean attractive?"

"He's cute but too nice," Kate said, grabbing a shot glass that said *County Galway, Ireland* on it. "Too touristy?"

Emily laughed, but knew Kate collected shot glasses.

Kate had one for every place she'd been and that amounted to a rather large collection. Emily also knew that if Kate thought Sean was too nice, he probably was. "I don't think Aedan's a jerk."

"Oh - yeah - Chef Aedan invited us to sit at the chef's table tonight for dinner. It's a four-course meal with some rather enticing selections. We absolutely have to go. I thought we'd get there around seven."

"There's no Irish stew involved is there?" Emily picked up an Ireland collector spoon along with one that said *Co. Galway* for her mother's spoon collection.

Kate shook her head and stepped up to the cash register. "No, it's not traditional Irish food at all. More like fine dining."

"Well for his sake I hope he cuts the meat properly." She pulled out her phone and looked at the screen. It was getting late. "I wonder if Sarah is still riding."

"I hope so," said Kate. She handed over the euros to the shop keeper. "The euro thing, it's so weird, isn't it?"

The woman behind the counter smiled, amused. "We're all used to it now."

When Kate was finished with her purchases, Emily stepped up with hers. "I think your chef is hot after you."

Kate's pale cheeks flushed pink. "Well, he can be interested all he wants. I think he's just trying to score a good review. Get his name in a magazine and put his restaurant on the international map."

"Who's being cynical now?" She paid for her purchases and gave the woman behind the counter a polite *thank you*.

It wasn't until they got outside that Kate decided to protest. "It would never work between a girl like me and a guy like Aedan. He's far too…"

"Nice?" Emily finished. "No, ambitious."

This confounded Emily. "You've dated stock brokers, news anchors, and minor celebrities…"

Kate shook her head. "I don't know. Besides, if I did flirt too hard he'd probably end up sleeping with my sister."

There on the sidewalk, in the middle of the small town of Kilnook, Emily broke out laughing and Kate followed. When the laughter wore down, they headed to the next shop in good spirits. They spent the afternoon browsing shop after shop. Kate picked up bizarre trinkets here and there and even grabbed a keychain for her sister.

It wasn't until Emily's watch alerted her it was ten to five that she frowned. The shops would be closing soon. "I'm going to text Sarah and see where she is. We should get back to the cottage and get changed if we're going to dinner by seven."

She sent the text from the car, and by the time they pulled into the cottage driveway, Sarah still hadn't texted back.

"Maybe we should call the stable," Kate suggested, looking worried.

It wasn't like Sarah not to text back immediately and both of them knew it.

Emily felt a deep pang of worry and once they were inside, she found the number to the stable and called. It rang twice before a woman picked up.

"Hi, I'm looking for my friend who rented one of your horses earlier? Her name is Sarah May."

"Yes," said the woman on the other end of the line. "We haven't heard from her either. I'm getting ready to send a rider after her now."

The skin on Emily's arms went cold with goose pimples, and dread sunk into her heart. "Thank you. Could you please call me once you hear anything?"

"Of course," said the woman.

Emily gave the woman her name and number and ended the call, vaguely aware of Kate looking at her with panic and fear.

"What is it?" Kate whispered.

"Sarah is missing," she said simply as if it was something that happened all the time.

That's when Kate went into panic mode. "How could this happen? How does someone just go missing?"

Dumbfounded, Emily just looked at her friend. "Don't panic. For all we know she rode a little further than she realized and when she noticed how late it was she turned around."

"What if she was thrown off the horse off a cliff or something?" Leave it to Kate to go to the worst case scenario right off the bat.

Emily was surprised she hadn't done the same thing. "No, Sarah's a good rider. She used to ride on her grandfather's farm growing up and she and Eric went on that riding trip…"

There was no way she'd accept that anything bad had happened to Sarah.

Emily's phone chime made them both jump. It chimed again, a ring tone that Emily found much more calming than a traditional phone ringer. "Hello?"

"We found your friend," the woman said, pausing.

The pause was far too long and Emily immediately braced for the worst.

"It seems she stopped to chat with one of the locals and lost track of time. She's on her way back to the stable now. I can have my husband drive her home," the woman said, her own voice filled with relief.

"Well thank God for that," Emily said, letting out a relieved sigh. "Thank you so much."

They said their goodbyes and Emily ended the call, looking at Kate. "She was hanging with the locals and lost track of time. She's on her way back now."

Kate breathed that same sigh of relief and started back toward the bedrooms. "Remind me to make polite mention how answering texts and making phone calls so no one worries are important."

"Noted," Emily said in agreement. "I guess we'll get ready and let's hope she gets here before we have to leave."

"We can wait for her. I doubt Aedan will give the table away. I'll call and let him know we'll be late if she's not here in the next half hour."

Emily agreed and both women went into their rooms to change for dinner.

Sarah showed up at ten to seven smiling ear to ear and happier than Emily and Kate had seen her in months. It was hard to be angry at her for not calling, but Emily made an exception.

"You didn't answer your text and we were worried sick," Em said. So much for a polite mention.

The blunt force of Emily's statement stopped Sarah in her tracks and she pulled her phone out of her pocket.

"Oh, I'm sorry. I forgot. I turned the ringer off because I was worried it would spook the horses."

Kate looked Sarah up and down and shook her head. "Well, I'll call Aedan and tell him we'll be about seven thirty. Sarah has to change."

"We got the chef's table at the local posh restaurant," Emily explained.

"Oh," Sarah nodded. Then she looked down at herself, realizing for the first time that evening that she'd spent the afternoon covered in dust and horse odor. "I'll go get ready."

"Did you at least have a nice ride?" Emily called after her.

"Yes, thank you. It was great. I'll tell you about it later," she said over her shoulder, hurrying to her room to bathe and change.

"We can't stay mad at her," Emily said, turning to Kate.

Kate nodded in agreement, then said offhandedly, "I wonder if we get the chef's discount, too? Any bets we don't?"

"Do you expect it?" Emily asked, checking herself over in the mirror one last time. They weren't dressed to the nines, but they were both wearing nice, summery dresses with evening jewelry. To be honest, Emily was worried they might be overdressed.

She shrugged. "Nope. But I am a food critic, so maybe?" Emily shook her head.

"What?" Kate gave her an innocent look then went into the kitchen to call the restaurant to let them know they'd be a little late.

Sarah emerged twenty minutes later ready to go. The three women filed into the car and were silent as Kate made her way into town in the pitch black of night. The Irish countryside was dark - a fierce dark impenetrable by the mere sliver of a waning moon. This ensured the darkness found every nook and cranny and yet by just the headlights of the car, Kate somehow found her way along the murky pitch roads into town. Outside *Mulligan's*, people milled outside on the sidewalk. From outside the pub next door, one could hear the traditional Irish band playing. They went inside *Mulligan's*.

They were promptly led to table in the kitchen and seated. From their vantage point, they could watch the entire kitchen staff going about their nightly work. Aedan noticed Kate immediately and winked at her.

It was official. Aedan was interested in Kate, and Kate was flattered, otherwise she wouldn't have accepted the dinner invitation. Whether or not they'd become an item remained to be seen. Emily wasn't sure Kate would give in if Aedan pursued her, but only because he wasn't Kate's type. Aedan wasn't a reckless millionaire or flippant player. He had a career and likely goals. He was the type of guy who settled down, bought a house, got married, and had a couple of kids. All things so foreign to Kate that it would never work.

Emily turned her attention to Sarah, who still had that dreamy, faraway look in her eyes. "The horseback riding that good?" Emily asked, taking a sip from the glass of water in front of her.

Before Sarah could answer, a petite blonde server came to their table with a bright smile that highlighted her blue eyes. "Tonight, Chef Aedan has a wonderful meal planned for you. Now, will each of you be having the wine to go with each part of the meal? Or would you prefer something else?"

"Oh, we're all doing the wine," Kate said. There was no arguing the point. Kate wanted her friends to experience the meal the way it was intended to be served.

"Wine's fine," Emily agreed. Sarah just nodded and smiled. "Very well," continued the server. "For your first course, you can have either the tomato and basil salad or the feta cheese mousse."

They all chose the salad.

"Next," the server continued, "You can have the cured and smoked duck breast or the cured salmon."

"I'll try the duck," said Kate, very excited.

Both Sarah and Emily wrinkled their noses. "Salmon," they both said in unison.

"You guys are chicken. You can try some of my duck if I can try your salmon," she suggested.

"Maybe," Sarah said with obvious wariness. "I'm not fond of duck. It's too fatty."

"For the third course," the waitress interrupted, "Loin of rabbit or sea bass."

After a long bout of silence, Kate volunteered, "They'll have the rabbit and I'll have the sea bass."

Sarah and Emily didn't argue.

"Finally, you can have either the cheese plate or a coffee and vanilla parfait." The server smiled expectantly and waited.

"Can we just get a cheese plate to share and the three of us each get our own parfait?" Emily asked.

"Oh yes!" Kate agreed.

At this point, Sarah was along for the ride and didn't argue with the selections. She still appeared to be far away.

"So what happened today?" Emily pressed, giving Sarah a little nudge.

"I met someone earlier," she said, all mysterious-like. Kate perked up. "A man?"

"A friend," she corrected. "His name is Kevin MacClery.

He has some horses. I met him while riding. He offered to take me out for a ride tomorrow to see a wedge tomb."

"Is that what they're calling it nowadays?" Kate asked with a coy smile.

Emily groaned. "Mind out of the gutter. Maybe he's just a nice guy who wants someone to go riding with."

"Thank you!" Sarah said, grabbing the glass of wine just poured for her by the table server. She took a mouthful. "It's not anything seamy. He has horses, which means I don't have to pay to rent a horse, and there are some places you can only get to by walking or on horseback. You guys are missing out... I told him I'd go."

Trying to hide her disappointment, Emily shrugged. "Well, tomorrow I think I'm heading out to a restored castle not far from here. Sean suggested it. Do you still want to come with me, Kate?"

Kate had forgotten.

"I was going to head to the next town over and check it out, but... I could go." It was obvious Kate preferred bustling town centers, not ruins or tombs.

"No, you go to the town. It's just as well. Sean said he'd drive me over," Emily said, swallowing the tart wine.

Would it be embarrassing to ask Sean to take her? He had offered, but maybe he was just being polite.

"You're scowling," Kate told her just as the salads arrived. "Oh, just thinking I should check the weather and be sure to wear a rain jacket. That goes for you both, too," Emily said, saving her disappointment. She didn't want to upset Sarah or admonish her for wanting to go riding. After all, it seemed she was in high spirits and that's exactly what Sarah needed. If this Kevin, his horses, and the promise of wedge tombs lifted her spirits, so be it. Emily could spend a day exploring a castle on her own. She certainly didn't want to take Kate if Kate was going to sigh and get impatient, wondering when they could get back to shopping and eating and spending idle hours lingering in the local markets.

Of course, she couldn't help but think a day with Sean might be uncomfortable, especially since he'd been flirting with her. She had to be mistaken. She wasn't the thin one. Sarah had lost around thirty pounds when Eric died, and Kate had always been slender, even when they were in college. The only person who carried an extra fifty pounds was her, and she was very self-conscious about it. Sam made sure of that.

They spent the remainder of the meal marveling at Aedan's cooking and comparing their adventures of the day, Kate being sure to not to mention Aedan, and Emily keeping Sean out of the conversation, too. Instead, they heard about Emily's walk on the beach, and Sarah told them all about the horses and the countryside and how she wanted to go for a beach ride, too. She even spoke a little bit about Kevin, but the details about the man were vague.

By the time dessert came, Emily found herself more curious. "So wait, you meet this guy out riding, you start talking and he just invites you back to his house?"

Kate jumped in then. "It's the Irish. They're super nice people. Earlier this morning while I was walking around town I had several invitations for drinks at the pub for tonight."

"Exactly," Sarah agreed. "I think Kevin was excited for a riding companion. That's all. He lives alone up there with a few hired barn hands and a housekeeper to keep him company during the day, but they go home at night. I think he just enjoys my company."

"I mean, how much do you really know about this guy?" Emily asked.

"You are *so* everyone's mother," Kate told her, then she finished her dessert wine.

"I'm just cautious. There's nothing wrong with being cautious." She frowned at Kate. That wasn't true, she didn't mother them, did she?

Sarah said nothing. She just smiled.

Aedan stepped up to the table with a grin and motioned to the near empty dessert plates. He addressed Kate. "How did I do?"

"Hmm, let's see." She was obviously flirting with him. Perhaps it was the wine. "I loved it. We all got to sample just about everything and I thought it was wonderful. What about you guys?"

Sarah nodded. "It was delicious. I enjoyed it."

"Me, too," Emily agreed, forcing a smile.

"Do I get five stars then? Perhaps a review?" That was certainly blunt.

Kate wasn't fazed. "All right. Five stars it is."

"I feel I should give you solid recommendations for other excellent dining spots while you're here," he said, wiping his hands absently on the towel he carried.

"You mean you actually think there are other good restaurants around here other than *Mulligan's*?" she asked, amused.

"I wouldn't be a good sport or a good host if I didn't suggest you sample a wide variety of cuisine while you're here. Life is too short to eat at the same place every night. I have Thursday night off, perhaps I should take you to one of my favorite restaurants in Galway, provided your friends wouldn't mind…" Aedan wore a sly smile.

"Well since you already have your five-star review it can't be because you're buttering me up," Kate shot back.

He laughed. "I'll see."

"Well let me know when you can. I'll need to make a reservation at least twenty-four hours in advance," he said. He winked at her. "Have a wonderful rest of your night, ladies. You're more than welcome to go into the pub from here."

"Thank you Chef Aedan," Emily beamed, then gave Kate a knowing look. "He's into you."

"We both just appreciate good food, that's all." That was a rather offhand dismissal for Kate. "So, should we go to the pub? I looked up local night clubs and there are a few in Galway we could go to this coming weekend."

Sarah cringed outwardly while Emily cringed inwardly. "Well, tonight I think I'd like to just go back to the cottage and maybe curl up on the couch and watch a movie."

With a slight intake of air, Sarah sat up straight. "That sounds nice. Let's!"

A deep sigh escaped Kate's lips as she relented. "Oh, okay.

A movie at the cottage it is."

After paying the bill, the three friends headed back to the cottage for a quiet night in. While none of them said it, each of them found herself feeling butterflies of anticipation for what tomorrow would bring.

10

Wedge Tomb

Kevin MacClery was a perfect gentleman. When he arrived at the cottage that morning to pick her up, he was friendly toward Kate and Emily and talked to them about their plans for the day while he waited for her.

"I hope you don't mind me taking her out for the day, this being a friends' vacation and all, but it's so rare I find someone to ride with," he was saying when Sarah emerged from the bedroom in a fresh pair of beige riding breeches, a light blue shirt and her paddock boots.

"I think it will be fun for her. I know how much she loves to ride and she doesn't get to do it much back home," Emily said, sounding like Sarah's mother.

Kate just nodded.

Sarah appeared in the doorway and Kate gave her a wide smile. "Well, we shouldn't keep you guys. I'm sure you'd like to get going."

Kevin's eyes followed Kate's and his head turned toward Sarah. Kate bounced her eyebrows at Sarah from behind him and nodded, a sure sign she thought Kevin was attractive. Emily gave Kate a playful swat and shook her head. Sarah laughed.

Confused by the laugh, Kevin turned around and looked at her friends. "I've missed something?"

"No, I just remembered something funny," Sarah lied. "Well then, we should go. The horses should be ready

by the time we reach the house." Kevin paused and nodded at Emily and Kate. "It was nice meeting you both and if we'll be late again, we'll be sure to call."

"I have my phone and I'll check it every so often, but remember that I'm turning the ringer off, so I don't scare the horses," she reminded them.

"Check," said Emily.

Kate just smiled brightly and followed them to the door to see them off.

Sarah felt much better once they were in the car, a sensible black Toyota Auris, driving away from the cottage.

"Your friends seem nice," Kevin said, his eyes steady on the road ahead.

"They are. I couldn't have better friends than Kate and Emily," she said, staring off into the distance. Her eyes looked beyond the scenery into her own memories. Kate and Emily had come through for her. During the funeral, at the wake... They'd protected her from all the sympathy cards and all the questions people had about Eric's death.

They'd kept her from insensitive comments made by people who didn't realize it was impolite to ask a grieving woman if her fiancé had at least made provisions for her in his will. Of course he had. Eric was a meticulous planner.

"Have I caused offense?" Kevin frowned.

"No... sorry. I was just thinking of all the things Kate and Emily have done for me in the past five months. I guess I feel kind of guilty leaving them to their own devices while I go out and have fun." There was no point in denying how she felt since Kevin seemed to be able to read her like a book. Perhaps it was because they had so much in common and he'd been where she was.

"Well, maybe what they have planned is fun for them, too." He frowned as a truck pulled in front of him, cutting them off. His hand came up instinctively across her chest to keep her from flying forward. "Sorry about that."

"Yeah, people drive kind of crazy out here." It was true, they did. There were a few white knuckle moments when they were driving from the airport that Sarah had to force herself to look out the window to the scenery beyond because she couldn't watch the road without thinking they were going to die thanks to speeding drivers. But she didn't say anything because she didn't want to seem like a terrified old woman.

"You should see them on unpaved roads," he said with a chuckle, and then he said, "Don't worry too much about your friends."

"No, you're right. They're fine and I think they're having fun.

Emily appeared excited to be going to the castle."

"Which castle is she visiting again?"

Sarah tried to remember the name of it. "Connag or something. I'm not sure."

"Ah, Castle O'Conghaile, that's a privately owned castle. The owner gives tours, though," he explained. "She must know someone who referred her."

"Sean. The man who owns the cottage. I think he gave her the information." That's when it dawned on Sarah that maybe that's why Emily seemed so evasive about her plans. She wasn't outright evasive, but she wasn't specific and that wasn't like Em. Usually, Em shared details or things she'd read, especially if she was excited and she had been excited about sightseeing. This time, Emily had been quick to accept Sarah's riding plans, and she'd even declined Kate's company. A half grin came over her, unbidden. She said aloud, "I think Emily is going to the castle with Sean."

Kevin gave her a strange look.

"Oh, we were wondering why she didn't seem too upset when I said I wanted to go with you today instead, and she didn't seem keen on Kate's begrudging willingness to go with her." When she realized it would require a lot more explanation than that, and she decided it wasn't worth it to torture Kevin with details of her friend's love lives, or lack thereof in Emily's case. With a quick head shake, she said, "Never mind. So why do people drive so crazy?"

Just like that, she changed the subject and on the rest of the way to his place, Kevin shared his theory about bad drivers, concluding they must be *gone in the head*. All of this said as he drifted into other lanes without a turn signal, and sped around other vehicles dangerously. Sarah decided to keep her opinion of *his* driving to herself.

The horses were saddled and their lunch packed when they arrived. Shadow stood next to a white mare.

Kevin led the way toward the mare. "This is Pickles."

"Pickles?" She couldn't help the smile.

"When she was young she got into some pickles and ate them. They're not good for horses. We thought she'd get sick, but luckily she didn't. She has a fondness for cucumbers, though, which may explain her love of pickles. So Pickles was the nickname that stuck. She was called Angel before that," he explained. "I think you'll find her easy-going."

After Kevin hoisted a pack onto his back and they checked the stirrup lengths and the saddle girths, they started off, but not toward the ocean path. Instead, they moved south, up gently sloping hills and back south-east, more inland, over grass covered hills. As they entered each new pasture, they had to open gates and close them once they were through.

"These are private property?" They followed the path along the emerald green fields, the morning dew glistening on blades of grass. "Yes. I know the property owners and they're fine with it. I have permission to ride through as long as I mind the gates," he said.

As they traveled through the beautiful countryside, she said aloud absently, "Imagine how many people never get to see Ireland like this."

"What?" He drew Shadow to a pause so Pickles could come forward.

"These are views you can't get from a car. These fields and this scenery - there aren't any roads here, so the only way you could get here would be by walking or riding a horse." As far as the eye could see, fifty shades of green glittered back at her. The clouds were clearing, showing a bit of blue sky beneath. She'd brought a rain coat just in case.

"It definitely is nice up here," he agreed.

Still, it felt odd for him to say *up here*. When most people said mountain, she expected to see a range like the Rockies. Instead, she was often greeted with older ranges that looked more like hills than mountains. Ireland was no exception to that. Their mountains were mere hills from her perspective.

They rode on, sharing childhood memories and stories about their first rides until they came to a lake.

Kevin urged Shadow straight into the lake and they started across.

A bit of fear ran through Sarah. She couldn't call Kevin back, she had to follow. If she fell in, she fell in. It wasn't like she couldn't swim. It was a wide lake, though, and getting dumped in the middle of it didn't sound fun.

"Come on," Kevin called. "To get to the tomb, we have to get to the other side. It's an extra hour to ride around!"

With a deep breath, she patted Pickles and urged her forward. "Okay, Pickles, I hope you can swim and won't flip out on me."

The horse twitched her ears and went into the water until the ground gave way beneath and Sarah could feel

Pickles strong withers move beneath her as the mare swam after Shadow. This was a new experience for Sarah since she'd never ridden a horse through a lake before. She was so enthralled in the sensation of such a new experience that it caught her off guard when Pickles found footing again and they found themselves in shallow water on the other side. Sarah looked back from where they'd come from. The opposite shore looked distant.

"You all right?" Kevin asked.

"Yeah, I've never ridden through water before," she said.

He winced. "I probably should have asked if you knew how to swim first."

"Oh, don't worry, if I didn't, I certainly wouldn't have followed you in," she assured him. "But that was pretty neat. I've never ridden a swimming horse."

"I'm glad to hear that. Next time, of course, stop me when I go on without asking obvious questions, would you?" he asked.

Sarah laughed. "I'll make sure of it."

They had to ride up trails through a heavily forested area before they rose above the tree line again. She guessed it was another two miles they'd ridden.

Finally, Kevin stopped and pointed to the summit of the hill they ascended. "There it is, our destination."

On top, she saw a stone structure that looked like a lean-to made of large slabs of rock. "That's the wedge tomb?"

He nodded. "They're usually not that far up. They're usually in the side of the mountain close to the top. But this one was put up top for some reason. Probably for the view."

They rode to the top and dismounted, dropping the reins. The horses were trained to ground tie and didn't move from where they were. First they took off the horse's saddles and set them on the ground next to a rock so they could dry. From his overstuffed backpack, Kevin produced two feed bags with grain. After removing the bits from the horse's bridles, he put on the feedbags. Sarah helped with what she could. The horses chomped happily on their lunch. Then he brought out a thin blanket that he spread out over the ground, and after that, he set out lunch.

Smoked salmon, soda bread, and chive butter along with two apples and two carrots.

"For the horses?" Sarah asked, hoping that was the case.

"The carrots are for the horses, the apples are for us." He sat down and took out a knife to slice and butter the bread. The salmon was already sliced into thin, delicate pieces.

Sarah felt famished.

"Oh, I almost forgot." Reaching back into the saddle bag, he pulled out a miniature bottle of wine and two plastic wine glasses. "Wine. We also have bottled water, of course."

She smiled and sat cross-legged on the blanket with him, looking up at the wedge tomb ten feet away. "So who's buried here?"

He shrugged. "Someone who lived over two-thousand years ago. They usually contain cremated remains, but it's anyone guess who they were. Could have been chieftains or warriors. Or perhaps princes or princesses. But whoever they are, may they rest in peace."

The wine had a twist top instead of a cork, and when he poured it, she was surprised to see it was red wine. Even with her limited knowledge of wine, she knew it was white wine that was often served with fish.

As if reading her mind, he said, "Pinot Noir goes fantastic with smoked salmon. Of course, this wasn't an expensive bottle, but it looked like it would travel well, and we didn't need much. I figured we should make a toast."

He handed her a plastic wine glass filled with wine and poured the remainder of the small bottle into his. With a reassuring smile, Kevin MacClery lifted the glass and said, "To new beginnings."

Yes, that's exactly what this was, she quickly decided. A new beginning. "To new beginnings," she repeated.

"This is it," Kevin said. "I don't think Eric would want you stopping your life, and you haven't. You're here, you've just ridden up a mountain to a wedge tomb, and now you're looking toward the future. The world is only dark if we allow it to be. We can choose to see the beauty and the light."

He motioned out over the landscape before them, the beautiful scenery in the rolling hills and farmlands below.

Deep within herself, she felt two things simultaneously that she hadn't felt in months. Hope and genuine happiness. Being here, on the top of a mountain, sitting by a wedge tomb with Kevin MacClery made her happy. For the first time in months, she had a future again.

"Now, you have to have some of this salmon, it's delicious." He cut thick slices of bread, buttered it, and placed several slices of salmon on top. He handed it to her and waited for her to take a bite. "What do you think?"

She tried one bite and took a sip of wine afterward before answering. "That's so good."

"So what's next?" he asked.

"I suppose we ride back down…"

He laughed. "No, I mean when you go back home."

Where that wouldn't have been an easy question for her to answer even yesterday, it was now. "When I get home

I'll have to finish packing the house and be moved out by the end of June so the new owners can take possession. I'll put all of Eric's things in storage until I'm in a place, mentally, where I could go through his stuff without bawling. Then begins the long process of finding a place I want to move to. I had a condo in mind."

"Oh, you have a buyer already?" He seemed surprised. "Well, I haven't heard from my realtor yet, but with the way houses are selling right now, I expect I'll have a buyer by the time I get home. I've got some equity in the house. Not much, but around twenty- thousand, which will be a nice down payment on the smaller place." With a shrug, she stopped talking. She didn't want to think about that right now, not when this place, and the company were both perfect. They sat in silence for a few moments.

"It's too bad you live so far away. I enjoy your company," he finally said.

"Me, too. But there's always email, social networking sites and the phone…" she started hopefully.

"True," he agreed, but added, "It's still not the same, though. I can't call you and say, hey, you want to go for a ride today?"

"Yeah, that does stink." A frown came over her lips. "I wish I could afford to have a vacation home here. I'd come out a few times a year."

"Well, if you're serious about that, I have a spare bedroom.

There's no need to buy a place when you have a friend."

She blushed. A man she'd only known two days was offering her a room in his house. What were the odds? "Oh, I'd never put that kind of imposition on a friend unless I'd known them for some time."

"What if I told you it wouldn't be an imposition?" He grinned at her and then turned his face toward the breeze, enjoying how it gently caressed his skin. "I could stay out here all day."

Looking up to the sky she could tell it was noon by how the sun stood high above them. More clouds appeared to be coming in from the ocean. "It might storm this afternoon."

"Well, in that case, we'll have to ride back and spend the rest of the afternoon at the house." His voice sounded almost lyrical.

"What will we do all afternoon?"

He shrugged. "Bide our time until dinner, and then I'll take you into Galway for dinner and dancing."

Her smiles were becoming more frequent. "That sounds fun."

"Well then let's do it," he said, his voice turning suddenly serious.

She noticed he hadn't shaved that morning and the five o'clock shadow on his jaw highlighted his already rugged good looks. Her heart sped up a little. *Slow down there, Sarah*, she told herself inwardly. It had been so long, though. So lonely. She couldn't deny that she longed for a man's touch, and not even in a sexual way. She just wanted to be held and told everything was going to be okay. Tears welled in her eyes and she turned away to regain control. The crying jags were the worst part of grief, she decided, because you never knew when they were going hit.

"Sarah?" His hand was on her shoulder. "Are you okay?"

"Just..." Her words were swallowed in a deep, ragged breath.

His arms went around her shoulders and he pulled her into his chest and his voice was low and soothing. "I know. The grief sometimes catches you off guard."

Breathing in the scent of him she relaxed against his chest, still fighting the sadness and comforted by his embrace.

"I'm sorry. I'm a mess. Maybe I should just go back to the cottage and take tonight to get back on track," she said. The truth was she knew how vulnerable she was right now, and she didn't want to fall for Kevin MacClery on the rebound. That's exactly what would happen if she allowed it to continue. She knew it.

"I don't think being alone and hiding from life is going to help. Instead of running away, you're running inside yourself and trapping yourself in your grief." He sounded solemn, like a man who was speaking from firsthand experience. He was.

"No, that's not it, Kevin." She turned her face up to him, realizing just how close his lips were to hers. "I think maybe I like you a little too much and I don't want to hurt you, or myself."

With that, she pulled away from him and stood. She crossed her arms over her chest against the wind and turned away, afraid to look into his eyes to see if she'd hurt his feelings. Or perhaps he was amused because he didn't feel the same way. It was always possible she was reading the signals wrong. Maybe Kevin did just want to be friends and was just trying to help her get over her depression.

Don't be stupid, Sarah. People don't go out of their way to help someone if they stand to gain nothing, her mind told her. Either way, there was no way this would turn out well - for either of them. She turned back to him.

Kevin bit his bottom lip and tipped his head to the side, looking at her as if weighing his words carefully. "I like you a lot, too, Sarah May. Don't run from this."

Drawing in another deep breath she finally let her eyes meet his. "What if what we're both feeling is just a rebound? What if things are going too fast? What if we hurt each other? What if," she paused because this was the scariest question yet, "What if it's too soon?"

She was on the verge of tears again, but she held them back. "What if it isn't? What if fate brought us together yesterday?

To hell with the what-if's! Sure, we don't know if we'll end up lovers and grow old together, or if we'll end up friends or bitter enemies, but don't we, at least, owe it to ourselves to find out? You can't deny there's a strong attraction between us and we'd be foolish to deny ourselves a chance at happiness," he said. "We've only known each other a day. It's not like we're committing to a long term relationship. Just a night out. For fun."

He was right. She was making this out to be far more than it was though his interest was clear. Kevin MacClery wanted to spend time with her to see if there was a relationship worth pursuing between them, and deep down it's what she wanted, too.

"Just say yes." His brown eyes danced with hope. "Okay. You make a good argument. We'll go." At that moment, she felt a surge of fear and excitement.

They re-saddled the horses and started back down the hill toward the lake, and the house. As they descended, Sarah knew in her gut she was making the right decision. She was finally taking charge of her destiny and taking her life back. Eric would have wanted it that way.

11

International Foodie

"I can see why Sarah was so dreamy last night," Kate said, looking over at Emily, who was putting together her bag for the day. "Are you sure you don't want me to go to the castle with you? We can get some shopping in afterward…"

"No, really, I think it would be fun to check it out by myself."

That was odd. It was rare Emily did anything by herself. "I just feel bad…"

Emily let out a sigh. "You're always the one telling me I'm not assertive enough, and maybe you're right. One of the ways to cultivate my assertiveness is to be independent. Do things by myself once in a while. Besides - admit it - you would be bored out of your mind."

With a shrug, Kate grabbed her own black bag and began checking to make sure it contained everything she'd need for a day of shopping and checking out local restaurants and markets. "Probably. Do you think this outfit is too New York?"

She motioned to the white pants, blue button-down shirt, and black blazer she wore, complimented by a pair of strappy brown sandals with two-inch wedge heels.

"It is a bit New York casual, but I think you can get away with it," Emily said. "How about me? Does my outfit scream castle tourist?"

Kate laughed. Emily, in jeans, a black t-shirt, and plain

tennis shoes looked just like everyone else. "You look normal."

"Are there times I don't look normal?" Emily said with a pretended frown.

Both women laughed.

"Do you want me to take you and drop you off?" Kate offered again, feeling bad for hoarding the car.

"No, I can catch a cab," she insisted.

"All right." She pulled her sunglasses from her bag and put them on. "I guess I'm heading over to Galway then. I'll scout ahead, check things out so I can find the best places, then we'll all go back together."

"That sounds fun," Emily said. "Have a great day!" Even as she was leaving, Kate couldn't help but feel Emily was holding something back. She wondered for a split second what was going on with her friends, but immediately dismissed it as her own paranoia. Sarah and Emily were grown women and the three of them had their own interests. They could easily spend time together as well as apart. At least this way they wouldn't be sick of each other by the time they headed home.

Once she made sure she had everything, she locked the cottage and went to the car. After dinner last night, Aedan had slipped her a list of some restaurants to check out in Galway. At the bottom, he'd written his phone number.

"If you have any problems at all, or you get lost, let me know," he said. There hadn't been time for them to discuss anything else. The restaurant was busy and he had diners to cook for.

The drive through Kilnook was quick and before she knew it, she was on a highway heading north, toward a village named Cleg. There, a restaurant called *The Gables* allegedly had the best-grilled prawns and scallop dishes on this side of the bay. According to Aedan at least. She figured she'd spend some time going through shops and taking in scenery, and by the time she'd seen the whole village it would be lunch time and she could check out the restaurant and maybe even the local pub afterward before heading back to Kilnook to pick up her friends for dinner.

So far the entire trip had been a huge success. Sarah was already smiling more and even Emily seemed to be enjoying herself. Of course, in a little under three weeks they'd have to go home. For Emily and Kate, it wouldn't be such a big thing. They'd go back to their busy lives feeling more relaxed, ready to conquer the world whereas Sarah had to go back to the house and pack it up. She and Emily had helped Sarah out by packing up Eric's things and putting them in the garage. The only thing they left was a single portrait of Eric in his dress uniform, on the mantel. All the pictures of Sarah and Eric had been packed up and put away, too. Not because they didn't want Sarah to remember him or how they were, but to limit the triggers that made her miserable, and seeing photographs of when they had been so happy caused Sarah to break down. Kate told her she could always take out the pictures and put them back up when she was ready. Sarah had agreed to that. But Sarah refused to take the one picture of Eric from the mantel, saying it wasn't right for her to just pack him off in boxes in the garage as if he never existed. Kate and Emily didn't fight her. They left the photograph there.

Being so far from home, she hoped, would make Sarah realize that life went on. Kate still found herself worried about Sarah, probably too much, but if riding horses was the thing that brought Sarah solace, she could ride every day for three weeks for all Kate cared. She just wanted Sarah to be happy, like she was before Eric died.

"Don't be stupid," she scolded herself aloud as two guys on Honda motorcycles blew past her. "Sarah will never be the same."

Saying it out loud made her realize that while Sarah could be happy again, she'd never be the same person.

There was no going back *before Eric*. Of course, this realization seemed to change how Kate viewed the entire situation. She'd been going about it all wrong. Now, instead of trying to help her friend get back to that place of happiness that existed before, she realized she needed to help Sarah find happiness now, in the aftermath. Of course Emily, who was worried in her own way, still felt Kate was intruding and worrying too much.

Em had her own problems, of course. Sam's abuse and infidelity turned Emily hard over the years. That emotional wall she put up made her appear unaffected by everything.

The sign announcing Cleg told her to turn left. Cleg, much like Kilnook, consisted of a main street and little else. At least Kilnook had twice as many shops. She pulled into a parking space at what appeared to be a corner store and turned the ignition off. Looking at her watch, she wondered how she would bide her time for the next two hours. It wasn't like there was a lot to do. With that in mind, she got out of the car and went into the small shop. Surely the locals would know what there was to do around here.

"Hi, is anything open around here?"

The woman behind the counter gave her an odd look and then smiled. "Most places don't open around here until ten."

"I was hoping to do some shopping before *The Gables* opened for lunch," Kate started.

"Well, you might get back on the N18 to Clarinbridge. Plenty of shops up that way to keep you busy for a few hours," the woman suggested. "I think you'll find more of them open than here."

"How long will it take to get there?" Kate almost felt like she should buy a little something to be hospitable. She took a bag of cheese and onion crisps from the display and set it on the counter. "I'll have these."

The woman smiled and rang up the crisps. "Shouldn't take more than fifteen minutes this time of day," she said. Kate handed her the money, received her change and took her crisps back out to the car with every intention of just leaving them in the cottage when she got home so if anyone needed a snack, they had something. She should have stopped somewhere for a light breakfast. Maybe some tea and toast. But if Clarinbridge was only a few minutes away, she might as well go there for a few hours, she decided.

The traffic flowed at a steady rate, surprisingly light for mid- morning, and she made it to Clarinbridge without any issues. The town bustled with people and it pleased her to see it was busier than the sleepy village of Cleg. There was certainly more in the way of shops here. She found a parking space and made sure to lock the car this time, then headed down Main Street to see what the town had to offer a mildly hungry, curious traveler who liked to shop.

The scent of fresh baked bread drew her directly to a small cafe called Claire's. Stepping inside a strong whiff of warm, yeasty, rolls fresh from the oven greeted her. An enticing display of pastries, scones, and breads drew her to the counter. Her eyes found the menu quite readily.

"Could I get some tea and lemon scones with apple ginger jam?" she said to the young woman behind the counter.

The woman nodded and got it for her, then returned to take her euros.

Kate thanked the clerk and carried her breakfast to one of the tables outside. A soft breeze promised a nice morning despite a few clouds. She could see blue bits of sky here and there, suggesting the gray day might clear up.

People watching was a favorite past time of the petite, blonde food critic. She ate her scone, loving the light, fresh lemony flavor mingled with the sweetness of the apple ginger jam. The scones were still warm and denser than she expected. They melted delightfully on her tongue.

"I should have figured you to be a scones and jam girl," a man said over her left shoulder.

She turned to find Aedan O'Byrne standing there. It was impossible to hide her surprise. "Oh, hi."

"You decided to take my advice and check out a few places here in Clarinbridge?" he asked, knowing full well she had taken his list seriously.

"I initially went to Cleg, but there was nothing there and it didn't seem much was open yet, so the woman at the small market suggested I come here," she told him, then asked, "Aren't you working today?"

"I don't always work. I'll be cooking tonight, but my time today is my own." He took the chair across from her without asking for an invitation. "Where are your friends?"

"Sarah went riding today, and Emily went to see a castle," she said. "I'm checking out various places, so I know what we're doing for dinner.

"Ah. So how many stars would you rate these scones?" She narrowed her eye at him. She'd met her match in Aedan O'Byrne. "I don't rate everything I eat by stars. They are good though. You want to try a bite?"

He reached over and tore off a piece of jam covered scone and popped it in his mouth. He chewed for a few seconds, then swallowed and nodded. "I say three of five stars."

"Pfft. More like four." A half smile came over her lips. "How do you figure? I think they used the wrong type of flour..." Now he was just mocking her and she knew it. "You're teasing me."

"All right, perhaps I am, but you were about to give my stew a bad rating just because a fatty piece of meat got into the pot." He leaned back and took her tea, and took a sip.

That almost set her laughing. She'd met a lot of arrogant men in her life, but none as brazen as Aedan. "So what are you doing in Clarinbridge today?"

"I'm surprised you take nothing in your tea."

"I'm from the mid-west. We don't do sugar in our tea.

Not even hot tea," she said, turning him back to the conversation. "Out for a shopping day?"

"Well, to be honest, I thought there might be a chance of running into you and your friends and I was hoping to show you around a bit. Seeing that you're alone, I'm glad I came." He shrugged as if following tourists around was something he did every day.

She knew it wasn't. Aedan seemed genuinely interested in her, even if it was for a favorable review. "Well, if you don't mind that I might do some shopping, then you can tag along."

He perked up and even seemed a little excited. "I know of a few shops you'll love. Then maybe we can have lunch and a bit of *craic*."

Her eyes went wide. "Crack?"

"It's an Irish word, it means fun, good food, conversation, that kind of thing," he explained.

Kate began laughing. "That is so *not* what crack is back home.

It's a very dangerous, illegal drug."

He laughed. "I imagine you'll be hearing lots of Irish words before you leave. Since you're in the *Gaeltacht,* you'll hear a lot of spoken Irish, too."

Not waiting for her to ask, he explained, "The *Gaeltacht* refers to certain areas where the Irish language is still used among the local population. We all still speak English, of course."

Kate nodded. "Well, then I guess I'm glad I'm with someone who can translate, so I'm not concerned that the locals are trying to get me hooked on crack."

He laughed again. "You might find yourself hooked on our kind of *craic.*"

They both laughed. Once she finished her scones and tea, they got up and started down the street.

The first stop was a meat market. Coolers and displays stood packed with fresh lamb, chicken, beef, and pork.

Aedan led her around the shop, pausing to look at some rabbit breast. Finally, he moved over to the fish counter and a display of smoked salmon. He handed her a package of smoked salmon. "That's good stuff right there. Shelf stable up to five years. Next, you'll need some Guinness whole mustard."

He found the shelf and held out a bottle. She took the small bottle of mustard from him. "So…"

"We're building you a care package to mail home to yourself full of irresistible Irish snacks," he said.

Both amused and intrigued, she followed him up to the counter. "Will all of this make it through customs?"

"Yes. I won't be sending you home with anything that will spoil or get you in trouble," he assured her.

She liked the sound of that. "Where will we be stopping next?"

"The cheese market for some gouda, aged cheese, and chutney." He seemed quite sure of himself. "A lot of people don't know this, but we have some cheese makers here who make award-winning Gouda. It shouldn't need refrigeration. And any aged cheese you get shouldn't need refrigeration until you cut into them anyway."

Taking his word for it, she followed him to the next shop, leaving with a locally made wedge of aged Irish cheddar, a wheel of locally made Gouda, and a jar each of locally made fig and apricot chutney, Ploughman's chutney, and red onion marmalade. After a while, her bags felt like they were filled with bricks.

She made him stop at a sweater shop so she could look at Aran sweaters, and then they stopped at a jewelry shop so she could get Claddagh rings for herself, Sarah, and Emily to remember their trip by. Aedan patiently waited while she browsed. She dragged him to the crystal shop and perfumery, collecting more bags as they went. Finally, they stood on the sidewalk and Kate realized she'd finished all the shopping for things she definitely wanted, which meant any shopping here on out was strictly for fun.

"Maybe we should put this in the car and then find a place for lunch," Kate suggested.

"All right," he said.

They took a long walk, uphill, back to her car, locked the bags in the trunk, and started back down Main Street again.

Aedan walked with purpose, knowing exactly where they were going and leading her to the *craic*. It was just after one in the afternoon.

So much for *The Gables*, she thought, but she didn't mind. Had she known this town had more to offer she'd have come here first anyway.

Together they entered a pub called *Nully's*, but instead of the rowdy atmosphere Kate expected, it seemed more upscale and low key. They found a table near the bar and sat down.

"Hey, are you supposed to be bringing the competition business?" she said suddenly.

"Ha! I like to think of it as checking out the competition. Research," he said, motioning to one of the servers for two beers. Likely Guinness. It was all about the Guinness here and that was fine with Kate, too. She wasn't normally a beer drinker, but Guinness was good.

The server put in their beer order with the bartender and brought them menu and said, "I recommend the fish butty or the beef sliders."

It was nice to see modern fare on the menu including quesadillas, fish and chips, and even fried chicken.

Surprising was more like it. She half expected more boxty, stews, and cabbage dishes. Ultimately she decided to have the fish butty. Aedan did the same.

When the beer came, she realized it wasn't the Guinness she expected.

"*Wicklow Wolf Black*," Aedan said, noticing the look on her face. "It's good, try it."

Taking a sip, she learned there was another beer she could add to her *like* list.

"There's more to beer than Guinness," he said in a whisper as if uttering those words aloud would bring Armageddon down upon them. Well, it was possible. "You have to trust me. I went to chef school and all that."

She leaned on the table with her elbows. "Well then, Mr. O'Byrne, where should we have dinner tonight?"

"Oh, you should definitely go to *The Gables* and have the scallops. They're award winning," he said.

The fish butty came and they ate and talked about capers and mayonnaise, and why fish tasted so good with lemon. By the time four o'clock and the second beer rolled around, Kate understood the meaning of *craic*. Aedan was interesting, charming, and they shared a love of food and all things culinary.

"You must have to write a lot to make a good living," he observed.

She shrugged. "Now that I'm well-known and have my own column in at least one publication, it's easier to get work. It was harder when I was a young writer just starting out. You never know where your next meal is coming from. I bet it's kind of the same way being a chef. You start by paying your dues as a line cook or prep cook and work your way up to having your own kitchen and your own menu."

"True," he agreed. "Now I spend all my time cooking, checking out restaurants, and going to culinary conferences."

"Yes! I'm covering a culinary conference in France two months from now. One of the magazines I work for is sending me," she said.

"The ICA Conference?"

"Yeah, that's the one."

"I'll be there, too," he said. "I just made my travel arrangements last week."

Kate remained engaged and leaned in toward him. "Well, I guess I'll see you there."

"I suppose so." His phone began beeping in his pocket and he pulled it out, looking at the screen with intense green eyes with golden brown flecks in them. "It looks like I'll have to go. We've run out of cream, so I'll need to stop by the dairy on my way in."

She frowned with disappointment. Their *craic* came to a halt. With a sigh, she stood. "Well, I should probably get back, too. Kate and Sarah will be wanting dinner."

They parted ways on the sidewalk outside of the pub. As she started back up the hill, Kate let her mind go over the day and before she knew it, she was at the car. The drive back to Kilnook took twenty-five minutes, and when she arrived at the cottage, she found it empty.

12

Tribes of Tara

Mrs. O'Flannigan sent Emily up to the barn because that's where Sean was. Walking up the path to the sizable outbuilding she wondered if he sheared the sheep himself. She didn't want to bother him for a ride if he was busy.

Doing his farm work was likely far more important than babysitting a tourist. If she could, she'd just see if he wanted to come along and if not, she'd call a cab.

Warily, she walked into the long barn, the rank scent of manure assaulting her nose. She grinned through it. Being on a farm was not something she'd ever experienced before. Inside, Sean O'Flannigan measured out buckets of grain.

"That's a lot of grain," she said, not wanting to sneak up on him.

He laughed. "I got a late start this morning. I have to feed the nursing ewes. Would you like to help?"

"Umm, sure?" Looking down at her jeans and tennis shoes she frowned. "Am I dressed okay?"

"I don't think they'll mind how you're dressed, as long as they're getting fed," he said, flashing her an amused smile.

"So do you raise them for wool?" She moved up alongside him, waiting for instruction.

His accent seemed thicker this morning than it had yesterday. "Wool *and* mutton."

She frowned at the mention of mutton. She wasn't a fan. Whether lamb or sheep, to her the meat always smelled like a damp sweater. It had an off-putting taste somehow, too. Kate, of course, had assured her that *properly prepared*, both sheep and goat were delicious. Emily never had any interest in finding out if Kate was right.

Turning her attention to the buckets, she put her hands on her hips. "So what do I do?"

"Set the buckets in the back of the cart," he said, handing her two buckets and motioning toward the golf cart.

"Why a golf cart instead of an ATV with one of those little trailers?" She was sincerely interested. Setting the buckets in the cart, she turned around to get two more.

He shrugged. "My father used to golf and had his own cart. I don't golf, so I figured it made sense to re-purpose it. Besides, it's not rough terrain and I've only gotten it stuck in the mud once or twice."

With a smile, she hoisted another two buckets into the back of the cart trying to imagine the strapping Sean O'Flannigan lifting the golf cart out of a muddy pool.

"Weren't you supposed to be going sightseeing today?" he asked.

"I am, just after I learn how to feed sheep," she told him. He laughed again. "Your friends ditched you again huh?"

She frowned. "They didn't *ditch* me. It was more like Kate would have been bored out of her mind and would have spent every moment looking at her watch and complaining that she was bored or hungry, and Sarah met a guy with horses, a Kevin MacClery, who promised to take her out to see a wedge tomb."

"Ah, MacClery." Sean nodded.

"You know him? He's not a psycho is he? Because if

there's any chance he might be a mass murderer or something…"

Sean chuckled. "God no. Poor man lost his wife awhile back. Cancer if I recall. He lives up in that big house all alone. He rides his horses around here often, so she's probably in good hands. I wouldn't have cause to worry."

"Well, I do worry. I think Kate told you part of the reason we're here. Sarah lost her fiancé in Iraq not too long ago," she started.

He nodded. "Yes, I know. Maybe it's good for her to be around someone who knows what she's going through."

"Oh." At that moment, it occurred to Emily why Sarah might be more interested in hanging out with Kevin MacClery than her friends. "That makes sense. She didn't tell us his wife had passed on."

Motioning her to get in the cart alongside him, he took the driver's seat. "No sense worrying too much about her. Mr. MacClery won't let any harm come to her. Now, are you ready to learn about feeding sheep?"

"Educate me!" She inhaled the scent of sheep and almost choked on it, but she recovered quickly.

Remembering back to how Sarah smiled at dinner the night before made her feel better. She and Kate had been worried all this time, but not once had either of them thought to suggest that Sarah join a support group. The answer was so obvious it hurt. It was exactly what Sarah needed. When they got back home she'd wait until Sarah was moved and settled and then suggest it to her. Perhaps she'd even find a few groups for Sarah to try out. There had to be other people out there suffering like Sarah was.

The slowing of the cart pulled Emily back to the task at hand. On either side of the road, alongside the fence were affixed feeders, but there were only sheep in the field to the left. She pulled out her phone and took a picture of the flock and quickly sent it to Lucy and her mother with the note, "Feeding sheep!" Then she slipped the phone back into her pocket.

He watched her over her shoulder, chuckled and exited the cart. Grabbing one of the metal buckets, he carried it over to the fence. "You just spread the grain out like this."

With precision, he distributed one bucket of grain over three to four feet in the feeder and the sheep that were dispersed in the field grazing on spring grass, started toward them. She grabbed her first bucket and followed suit. It only took a couple more trips back to the feeder with filled buckets before all the buckets were empty and about thirty ewes were happily munching grain. The spring lambs seemed wholly unconcerned by the process since they were still suckling. Sean proceeded to check the water troughs to make sure they were filled. On two, he had to turn on the hose.

"So what do you think? You want to be a sheep farmer?" His voice teetered on the edge of amusement.

"I could probably do it," she said, matter-of-fact, noticing all of the sheep had all of their wool sheared already. "My daughter, Lucy, would love it. She loves animals."

"It's the most work during shearing and lambing season. They don't need grain usually. Only the ewes, when they're pregnant or nursing," he explained, motioning to the flock of sheep. "They do all right otherwise. So if you don't mind me running in to change my clothes at least, I'd like to take you to that castle…"

"Oh, I don't want to be an imposition. I can take a cab.

I just wanted to say hello and thank you for your help yesterday," she lied, "And see the sheep."

He saw right through that. "It's not an imposition. I wouldn't have offered if I wasn't prepared to follow through. I would like to show you around."

His smile was genuine. Once he was satisfied the sheep looked okay, they climbed back into the white golf cart and headed back to the barn.

She only had to wait ten minutes before he exited the house dressed in a fresh pair of jeans and a clean shirt. She was pretty sure he'd changed his shoes, too. They got into the truck, now without the straw bales, and he turned around in the drive, heading toward town.

"It's a good day for getting out and seeing the sights," he said, trying to start up more conversation.

"Yeah, it is, isn't it?" Looking up to the sky it was overcast, but the temperature was still comfortable. It appeared the sun could break through the clouds at any moment. Her thoughts drifted briefly to Lucy and her mom. They were likely still asleep.

As if he could read her mind he asked, "So how are your mother and daughter getting on without you?"

Em shrugged. "Well, I'm pretty sure bed times have been slack and junk food is being had, but otherwise, my mom runs a tight ship. Lucy's still in school until mid-June, so there's homework to be done and all that."

"How old is your daughter?" He sounded genuinely interested. She wondered then if he'd ever wanted his own family.

He wasn't getting any younger, and men sometimes felt those pangs of wanting children, too, didn't they? One of these days she'd have to ask a man that question. It was also entirely possible he did have kids and she was just assuming he didn't. "She's twelve, going on thirty as the saying goes."

"Ah. Is that the age where they become all-knowing?" Laughter tumbled from the back of her throat.

"Something like that. They know everything and their parents are just trying to ruin all their fun. Which I suppose is true to some degree. But only because we've been there, right? We don't want our kids to make the same mistakes we did. With hindsight being twenty-twenty and all that."

"I don't have kids of my own, but I'd like to have them some day." A calm smile sat on his lips, unmoving. He seemed serene and not in a hurry to get anywhere. Emily knew then and there that Sean O'Flannigan *wanted* to be there. With her.

"I would say you're missing out, but parenthood is hard. Don't get me wrong," she said quickly and looked at him in earnest, "I love Lucy, but I almost wish I'd…"

Her voice cut off. What did she wish? Did she wish Lucy had never been born? No. Lucy was one of the best things that ever happened to her. She wished Lucy had a different father. One who appreciated his daughter. Who appreciated the wife who made sacrifices for their marriage, his career, and their daughter.

"Go on," Sean said, his interest in evident.

"I wish I had waited to get married, and that Lucy had a different father." That answer satisfied her because it was the truth, no matter how ugly that truth was.

Her answer seemed to satisfy Sean, too. "Certainly he wasn't *that* awful when you married him."

"He hid it well," she said, looking down at her hands. It was embarrassing admitting she made such a lousy choice in a husband. "He was fine until I gained the weight."

"What's wrong with your weight?" he asked. "I don't understand this obsession with weight people have. Doesn't matter how many stone you are." He paused as if choosing his words carefully. "I think you're lovely just as you are."

Her cheeks flushed crimson. "Thank you."

"No really, I'm not just saying that. You're an attractive woman. He was stupid to do whatever he did to cause the divorce."

"Well, aside from being emotionally abusive, he decided to have an affair," Emily admitted.

"That's what you meant then, when you said he didn't think family was important." The fact that he'd remembered their conversation from yesterday made her smile. He'd actually listened to her.

"The people we hurt are the ones we love. It's easier to lash out at them because we think they won't run away." Never were wiser words spoken than what came out of Sean's mouth. He frowned then. "But it's good you were able to get out of that relationship, especially if it was *that* bad."

"I think Lucy and I are better for the divorce," she said, searching for a way to change the conversation to something more upbeat. The air in the cab turned uncomfortable so she rolled down the window. "So what about you? You know my story. Woman gets married, has baby, husband turns out to be an ass, finds a girlfriend, and throws wife to the curb. What's your story? Aside from being the unexpected, smart scientist who moved home to help his mom with the farm after his dad died…"

Sean took to her invitation graciously and let out a long sigh. "There's not much to tell. It seems I always pick the women who haven't settled down yet, and I've always been settled."

"Hmm." She fidgeted with the seatbelt, pulling it off of her neck. Later she'd have to adjust it or it would drive her crazy on the ride back. Whoever sat here last must have been much taller. Finally, she said, "You sound like my friend Kate. Always dating the party animals and players.

Of course, she's not settled. I think she'd like to be, she just doesn't know how."

"I heard she and Aedan had a run in." His tone wasn't judgmental. Instead it sounded like a passive observation.

"News travels fast in Kilnook."

"It always has. But Aedan is a good bloke. He's too ambitious for most women, but your friend Kate is rather ambitious," he said. That *almost* sounded like a question.

Emily's eyebrow lifted in reflex. "Are you suggesting Aedan likes Kate and maybe they'd make a good couple?"

"Or at least a vacation romance." He shrugged.

A brief surge of annoyance ran through her. "Is that what single female tourists are? Potential *vacation romances?*"

"I didn't mean it that way. It's just that when you live in a small town like this, meeting new people can be difficult unless you travel a lot or use those dating sites and drive thirty miles to take a woman you've never met to dinner.

When there aren't a lot of local prospects, yes, you do consider the attractive single female tourists as potential partners." They'd just driven past town and were headed northwest, toward Galway Bay.

Before she could open herself to respond, he said, "And I don't mean sex. I mean potential relationship material."

"Knowing that they'll only be here a short time?" She wasn't buying it.

He shrugged again. "A lot of the female visitors we get are Irish women from different parts of the country. Some from Dublin. Sometimes they're foreign students. It's not unheard of for a long distance relationship to work. Or for a man or woman to move to be closer to someone."

"Well, then you must be a hopeless romantic. Am I right?" That was the only reasonable conclusion she could come to.

"In my spare time, and sometimes on Fridays." She could tell he was fighting back a laugh.

"Sorry if I got a little cranky, I'm just sensitive. That happens when you were married to an ass for twelve years."

Her eyes traveled to the scenery passing. She could see a large body of water ahead, but she wasn't sure if it was a lake or the bay itself.

"Fair enough. I was just trying to say that Aedan is respectable and if he is genuinely interested in your friend, Kate, he will treat her honorably." His voice had an earnest tone to it.

"Well, I wish Kate would settle down with someone.

Maybe that is the secret, she needs a man who lives in another country. That way her sister wouldn't sleep with them." It sounded good in theory.

Sean chuckled. "Sounds like she's had a time of it."

"We're all screwed up. You've got three screwed up American women renting your cottage." A frown covered her lips as she realized the truth of what she said. Every last one of them was damaged in ways that likely required counseling and possibly drug therapy.

"I much prefer that than a cottage full of frat boys, or a boring church group." His eyes stayed on the road as it became curvier and they began descending the hill. "Besides, none of the people we usually rent to let me go sightseeing with them. I haven't been to the castle since we helped the owner move some things in."

"Really?"

"The locals are usually the last people to visit places

frequented by tourists. I'm sure it's the same where you live."

Emily nodded. He was right, there were a lot of touristy things she'd never done in Denver. "I live in Colorado and I've never skied a day in my life. I've never been to Buffalo Bill's grave site either. Passed it on the highway a few times."

"Well, perhaps someday I'll visit your town and you can take me sightseeing."

Knowing that would never happen, she agreed. "You've got yourself a deal."

They rounded a bend and that's when she saw Castle O'Conghaile, its spires rising high above the rocky crags of the cliffs below. The body of water was definitely the bay.

"This is so incredible and beautiful." She couldn't take her eyes off how amazing it was. There was no way to get a good picture while they were moving. "Could you stop on the side of the road so I could send Lucy a picture?"

"Of course." Immediately he pulled the truck off to the side of the road. "You want me to take it?"

Since he was in a better position, she agreed and handed him her phone with the camera screen cued up.

Thank goodness he wasn't technologically challenged.

He took the picture and handed the phone back to her. "How's that?"

Upon seeing the picture, she smiled. It was perfect. She sent Lucy and her mother the picture with the caption, "Going to a castle!"

"Have they been enjoying your pictures?" Carefully, he pulled back onto the road and they were moving again.

"Yes. I send the pictures as I've been taking them and for the last few nights I've sent Lucy a small summary of what I did that day." Right then she realized that she felt relaxed. Talking to Sean felt like talking to an old friend, and for some reason - she felt like she could tell him anything.

They drove the next few minutes in silence, enjoying the scenery and the moist, salted ocean air.

Finally, they reached a parking area and Sean got out, greeting a man who exited the garden to meet them.

Once she was out of the car, Sean called her over, "Emily, this is Mr. O'Byrne. Aedan's father. He and his wife own this haunted beast."

"It's not haunted," the man said with a smile. He took her hand and shook it. "My wife and I are restoring her.

She was practically falling to ruin up until five years ago."

"This isn't a tourist type castle?" she asked, confused. "Oh, we give tours all the time. It helps pay for the renovations," he explained. "We simply cater to smaller groups. Are we waiting for anyone else?"

"No, it's just us. I thought I'd come take a look, too. I haven't seen it since you bought it." Sean looked up to the tallest turret. "That one was crumbling last time I was here.

"We had all of that fixed first. You don't need to be walking below and have a piece of stone fall and crack you on the head." He motioned them to follow him and hollered, "Meg, we have guests. Could you put the kettle on?"

"Who is it then?" a woman's voice called back. "Sean O'Flannigan and a lady friend." Mr. O'Byrne winked at her.

A short, stocky woman with dirty blonde hair pulled up in a loose bun came out to greet them. "Sean, I haven't seen you in some time. How have you been?"

"I've been well, thank you Mrs. O'Byrne. The sheep and my mother keep me busy." He gave the woman a pleasant smile.

"Well, hopefully not too busy," she commented, looking over his shoulder at Emily.

"This is Emily…" Sean offered.

"Emily Frost," Emily finished, feeling shy. It felt like they were intruding on these people's lives, but she knew it wasn't true when Mr. O'Byrne came back.

"All right then, come along, I am looking forward to showing you the renovations I did on the second floor and on the allures. Not to mention the turrets." He seemed genuinely excited.

"Enjoy the tour," Mrs. O'Byrne said sweetly. Emily gave her a polite nod. "Thank you."

She followed the men, feeling horribly guilty because they hadn't paid for a tour yet, and that was how these lovely people afforded to fix up the amazing castle.

She finally found the courage to say something. After all, she didn't want to appear disinterested. "What's an allure?"

To her, it sounded like perhaps he meant the castle was alluring.

"A walkway along the top of the walls," O'Byrne said without missing a beat.

"Do you live here full time?" she asked.

"Oh yes!" Mr. O'Byrne said. "There's a lot of history in these walls. Castle O'Conghaile dates back to the thirteenth century. It wasn't always called Castle O'Conghaile. It was built by invading Normans and eventually fell into Irish hands. It's been through a lot of restorations and renovations over the years, of course. The last owner called it Castle O'Conghaile because that clan belonged to one of the original Four Tribes of Tara. Lots of Connolly's in Galway to this day."

"Why didn't they keep ownership of the castle?"

"It's a lot of work to upkeep a castle like this. It's also expensive. A lot of people these days don't have the time, the money or the desire to continue on. Very few of them are held by private individuals these days."

"I've often wondered that myself," Sean said. O'Byrne shrugged. "People move."

Emily found Mr. O'Byrne's comment funny, but her amusement was cut short when she realized the interior of the castle looked quite modern. One of the walls appeared to be dry walled and modern family photographs hung there. There was even a flat panel television on an extendible arm attached to one wall across from a modern living room furniture set.

"This isn't usually part of the tour. Since Sean is practically family, I saw no harm coming through the house," explained Mr. O'Byrne, noticing her confusion. "Meg would have killed me had I insisted she live in an authentic humid medieval castle without modern plumbing. Usually, I take the guests through the side door, through the part of the castle that has been restored, but isn't lived in. We keep part of it original for historical purposes."

"Oh." This put a whole new dimension on things.

Sean reached out and gently guided her forward with his hand on her shoulder. Her heart quickened and she felt a surge of excitement run through her. No man had caused that kind of reaction in her since she was in college. Taking a deep breath, she composed herself and together, she and Sean followed Mr. O'Byrne on the tour of the castle.

13

Beneath the Stars

Once the castle tour was over, Mr. O'Byrne led them to a cobblestone patio with wrought iron table and chairs. The chairs had beige cushions and she, Sean, and the O'Byrne's sat and enjoyed the brackish light breeze. His wife brought out tea and biscuits. Emily smiled knowing exactly what Lucy would say if someone brought her biscuits and they were actually cookies. *"Cookies are biscuits?"* she would ask.

God, she missed Lucy, though she never expected it to hit her so hard. She thought she needed a break from her responsibility, but the reality was she just needed a break from having to spend the bulk of her days with co-workers who likely didn't care if she lived or died.

"There's nothing like that air," the older man said with a contented smile. His comment pulled her out of her own head.

Sean nodded. "It reminds me, I spend too much time at home and in town."

"You should get out more. Luckily this pretty lass found you." Mr. O'Byrne winked at her.

Emily blushed a little. Just what did Mr. O'Byrne think was going on between her and Sean? Who was she kidding, she knew exactly what he thought. He thought she and Sean were a couple, and in this moment - so they were.

He wasn't denying it or correcting the chatty castle owner or his wife, so she saw no reason to. What she wanted to do was slip away to the powder room so she could freshen up and sneak a few photographs to Lucy and mom. The pictures from the top of the battlement walls were breathtaking and she just knew the photos would send Lucy's imagination soaring.

"May I use your toilet?" she asked. It still felt strange to ask for the toilet instead of the bathroom, but it was one of the many things Kate stressed that Emily and Sarah would need to get used to for the next three weeks. Toilet, as a word by itself, seemed so undignified. Even unladylike. Of course, that was probably that Puritan cultural thing most Americans had going on when it came to sex, farting, and the fact that everyone poops.

"In the door here, straight across, and right into the bog," Mr. O'Byrne said, pointing.

His wife groaned at his instruction and got up, leading the way. "Sorry about my husband. He doesn't always have manners."

"Oh, no, it's okay. Your hospitality has been wonderful." Emily nodded her head a little.

Mrs. O'Byrne showed her right to the restroom door and left her. Once alone, Emily made sure she had a good cellular connection and sent a few of the castle photos. A response text came back immediately from her mom's number.

"So jelly!" it said.

Emily smiled. It was Lucy, and this was the first time she'd spent away from Lucy this long.

Knowing she would be missed if she stayed much longer, she rinsed her hands, made sure she looked presentable, and left the sanctuary of the toilet to rejoin Sean and their hosts. She didn't want to be rude.

Another text came in as she neared the door leading to the patio, so she paused to check it.

"Maybe next time U go 2 Ireland I can go 2!" Lucy typed. Sean poked his head in the door. "Everything all right?"

Emily shook the phone at him. "Lucy. I sent a few more photographs and evidently she's *jelly* and wants to come with me next time I come."

He gave her a broad smile, "Jelly?

"It's young people slang for jealous," she explained.

Her knowledge of American teenage slang seemed to grow more and more each year. Of course, fluency in slang wasn't something one could really brag on.

"Well, jelly just makes me hungry, want to get going and find some dinner with me?" Sean gave her a hopeful look. How could she say no to that face?

Just then, the phone chimed again. Lucy sent her a *selfie* with a goofy smile on her face, making Emily miss her even more. After sending a quick heart with some X's and O's, she closed the text message window and noticed there was an unopened message there. She hadn't noticed it before. It was a half hour old and it was from Sarah. Evidently Sarah had other plans for dinner. Perhaps Kate wouldn't mind if she bailed out, too? "Let me check with my friends to see if they mind."

"All right." Sean left her to it and went back to their hosts. "OK. I'm having dinner with Sean," she texted to the group.

Only Kate's response seemed upset, or maybe Emily imagined it. You could never tell with Kate. She was often abrupt. Besides, Kate always made so many friends wherever she went and always had plans for things to do that it was doubtful one night left to her own devices would draw her into anything inappropriate. Plus — Kate had the car while Sarah and Emily resorted to hitching rides with men in exchange for dinner. She laughed at her own joke, but decided to keep it to herself just in case it wasn't nearly as funny as she thought. She texted a quick assurance to Kate that they'd have dinner tomorrow.

Stepping out onto the patio and closing the door behind her, she turned to the O'Byrne's and apologized. "I'm so sorry about that. I don't usually use the phone that much, but my twelve-year- old daughter wanted to chat a little. I think she misses me."

"Oh isn't that nice. They're still sweet at that age, aren't they?" Mr. O'Byrne didn't wait for an answer and quickly asked, "So where are you two off to for dinner then?"

His wife shook her head, but then gave Emily a reassuring smile.

"I was thinking maybe we'd head over to Lisdoonvarna and Mary's and see the Burren and cliffs on the way," Sean told him.

"Nice clear evening for that. Better make it to the cliffs before seven or it will be black as pitch and you won't see much," he said. "Then I guess we should go then. Thank you for the tour and the tea, and the use of your toilet. I love what you've done with the place." Sean hugged Mrs. O'Byrne and then Mr. O'Byrne and in a flurry of goodbyes they left the castle behind them, heading back inland to find a road that would take them to Lisdoonvarna, and the places Sean wanted to show her.

"You know the O'Byrne's well?" Yes, it was a prying question, but she wanted to know.

"I went to school with Aedan O'Byrne and we were always at his house or mine. He knows my mum just as well as I know his."

This was the first time he'd used *mum* instead of mom or mother in front of her. A sure sign he felt relaxed around her, or she hoped. Emily tried to imagine a young Sean and Aedan running around the green hills of Kilnook carrying sticks and finding streams and forest groves to play in. There were certainly enough of them around. She sometimes wished she grew up in such a majestic small town instead of the sprawling suburb along the front range of the Rocky Mountains that was Denver.

"You're smiling," Sean commented. "It's nice to see you smile."

"I do it often," she said defensively.

"No, not always. You often seem rather serious."

She felt her face contort into a frown as she pondered this. "See," he pointed out.

This made her laugh. "Fair point. I was smiling earlier because

I was trying to imagine you as a boy playing in those fields around your house."

"Well maybe if you come up to the house my mum will show you the photo albums." He shook his head, trying to hide an emergent grin.

"I think I'd enjoy talking to your mother," she told him in all seriousness. "She seems like a nice lady. Maybe even a bit lonely."

"Don't let her convince you of that. She goes to church every Sunday, has tea with her friends at least once a week, and still finds her way into town for a pint at the pub at least once a week." He paused long enough to safely merge onto a main thoroughfare. "Also, don't let the sweeping fool you. We have the cleanest porch this side of Galway Bay for a reason. She uses sweeping as an excuse to pry, engage people in conversation, and lure them into the house for tea."

Emily laughed.

"You think I'm humoring you, but I'm dead serious.

My mum is crafty like that," he said, then he switched gears.

"We should check out the Burren and the cliffs while it's still light outside."

"So what is the Burren exactly?" Emil wanted to ask earlier, but didn't because she didn't want to sound like an idiot.

"Many kilometres of water soluble rock. Limestone. It's a fascinating landscape. It used to be a sea millions of years ago. I guess there are lots of fossils in the rock, but I haven't personally seen any." He shrugged. "It's kind of a big deal around here because it draws a great deal of traffic."

"You know quite a bit about geology. Or is this common knowledge for someone born here?" She welcomed the academic conversation because it took her mind off the fact that she found Sean attractive.

"Not really. I took a geology course in college, but we came here when I was in primary school. It left an impression," he said, sounding rather serious. "Had I not gone into biochemistry and molecular biology, I might have become a geologist."

"Do you miss it?" A melancholy feeling came over her. "What?"

"Working in a lab? Being a scientist?" Try as she might, she couldn't imagine him wearing a lab coat doing science-stuff.

He shrugged. "Sometimes. But the farm is important to my mother and I want her to be able to live in her house until her dying breath if possible."

The weight of his words seem to suck all of the air from the cab of the truck. "But surely if you wanted to still work in a lab you could, and make more money than if you ran the farm. So you could still afford to keep your mom's house for her."

"If there were labs around here hiring, certainly.

Unfortunately, that's not the case. I could sell the farm, work and live someplace else, and leave my mother to it, but who will take care of her when she gets old?" His sense of duty humbled her. "I don't like the idea of her spending years alone in the house while I live someplace else."

At the sacrifice of your own life, she silently added. Emily wondered then if she could do the same for her mother when the time came. After all, when she and Lucy moved in it wasn't to help her mom, it was so Emily and Lucy wouldn't have to live in a tiny apartment after the divorce. It was for Emily's emotional comfort. Her marriage fell apart and she immediately ran home to her mother like a child. Never mind that her mother probably enjoyed having them there. At that moment, she felt like the most selfish and childish person in the world.

Letting out an audible sigh she said, "You either have to be the most responsible and wonderful son in the world or a complete sadist."

"Sadist?" His confusion was evident.

"You sacrificed your entire career, your life, your dreams to take care of your mother and the sheep." She bit her lower lip and decided to be honest. "I don't know if I would do that for my mom."

"I don't see it that way." Luckily her comments didn't appear to offend him. Instead, he took the conversation in stride. "Sure, I am still paying off student loans, but I like sheep just fine and my mother is easy to live with. Family and friends, that's what's important in life. So I may never work in a lab or live alone, I don't mind it. My mum is respectful of my privacy. I have my own entrance to the house around the back, and I let her live her life. It's nice to have privacy but to not be alone somewhere."

"So I guess that means you have women over." As soon as the words came out of her mouth she wanted to crawl under a rock, and from the looks of the landscape stretching out before them, she had plenty of rocks to choose from.

He held out his hand as if presenting something, "I give you *The Burren*."

She bit her lower lip again, wondering if he'd heard her. "It's very rocky. You weren't kidding."

"And yes, in the past I *have* entertained a woman in the house when my mother was home. My apartment is partitioned off. Though admittedly it's been a few years." The suggestive smile that followed caused Emily's cheeks to flush crimson.

He pulled the truck off into a parking area.

Her eyes traveled over the rocky terrain. While there were all kinds of plants flourishing between the cracks in the limestone, the karst landscape went on for miles.

Beyond it, she could see the ocean. She got out of the truck and stepped out into the cool wind. "Wow."

Sean followed.

After snapping a few photos for Lucy and mom, she turned to Sean. "This is so much more incredible than I thought it would be."

"I knew you'd like it." His voice boasted self-assurance that made her smile.

"Can we walk around?"

He looked at his watch. "We only have about forty-five minutes to sunset. I'd much rather you see the sunset from the *Cliffs of Moher*. Lucy and your mum would like that picture a lot. Here, give me your phone and I'll take a picture of you standing right over there."

She handed her phone over and stood out near the entrance to a trail leading through the rock.

"All right. I've gotten it." He went to her and stood next to her, putting his arm around her. "Now a Sean and Emily *selfie*."

Emily laughed and the picture that resulted showed a rather attractive couple having a great time. They got back into the truck, heading toward the cliffs. As they went, Emily forwarded three photos, one of *The Burren*, one of her standing there with *The Burren* overwhelming the landscape behind her, and the smiling photo of her and Sean.

The Cliffs of Moher were even more amazing. The view took Emily's breath away. She'd seen some beautiful places before, but nothing like this. The only place she'd seen scenery this pristine was in movies. She took a series of photographs, then Sean took a picture of her, and another couple obliged them and took a picture of her and Sean.

Behind them, the sunset gleamed at them like an orange fireball on the edge of the ocean. Never before had there been such a perfect moment in her life captured in a picture. Therefore, she was certain that whatever happened between she and Sean was doomed to fail, so she might as well enjoy it while it lasted. She had a little over two weeks to bask in the fantasy. Hopefully, it didn't go horribly wrong before then.

They made it to Lisdoonvarna and dinner fifteen minutes after the sun set. There was a contented silence between them until they were seated inches from one another in the modern style booth of the restaurant. While the place was called *Mary's*, it had an additional Gaelic name that Emily couldn't pronounce.

"Two pints of the black stuff," Sean told the waitress. Emily's eyes went wide. "What's that?"

"I assumed you liked Guinness since you were drinking it in the pub back home," he explained, clearly worried he'd made a mistake.

"Oh, yeah. I just haven't heard it called that before," she explained with a shy smile. The napkin in front of her became the focus of her attention and she began to fold over the end, rolling it onto itself.

"I don't know if I understand you, Emily Frost." He tipped his head to one side and looked at her thoughtfully.

"What do you mean?"

"One minute you seem open and happy, the next moment pensive, and then you become shy and closed. It's like you want to open up but you aren't sure…"

She knew he was right. She could see it on his face, in his gray eyes. Those eyes, they saw through her to the core of her.

"Well, twelve years in a verbally abusive relationship does that to a woman," she told him as the waitress returned with their beers. They ordered steamed mussels and clams with vegetables.

Sean didn't have much to say to that. After the waitress left, his lips drew into a grim line. "For his sake, I hope I never meet him."

Emily decided to change the subject to something lighter. "So how long does it take you to shear all those sheep?"

"I usually hire some of the young lads from town for a few days and we shear the sheep morning to night until we're done." He took a swig of beer. "You're not truly interested in sheep."

"I am." Indeed, she was. "In my head, I glamorize farming and animal husbandry. I see it as the simple life even though I know better. I know it's hard work, but it's such a change of pace from the nine-to-five office nonsense I put up with, that I think I would welcome feeding and shearing sheep. Even mucking out a barn. That kind of physical activity would certainly take me back to my pre-baby, pre-low self-esteem weight."

His eyes examined her beer glass. She looked down, too. She'd only drank a third of it. While true that alcohol did make her speak her mind - that was all it did.

"No, I haven't had too much to drink. A few mouthfuls of beer hardly gets me drunk," she assured him with a laugh. "I just don't want to dwell on that *asshat* I married."

Asshat was a word Lucy introduced her to. Emily wasn't that thrilled about Lucy's use of it, but it fit Sam rather well.

Her chosen description made Sean smile. "So what should we do after dinner?"

"Pfft. I'm going to have to call it a night I'm afraid.

Which is too bad because I'd love to see your apartment. I have a sneaking suspicion Kate felt jilted tonight. Which means lots of friend-time tomorrow." She let out a heavy sigh.

Sean's smile grew, but he didn't blush, he just leaned in and licked his lips. "So are you saying you want to spend the night with me?"

She felt the heat rise in her cheeks. "Mr. O'Flannigan, I'm not that kind of girl. At least not tonight."

He leaned back in his chair, still smiling. "Very well. What about tomorrow night?"

With a coy shrug, she said, "Maybe the day after tomorrow?"

They flirted through dinner, but once they got back to the truck, conversation turned serious again.

"You probably should spend more time with your friends. I should be the least of your concern," he seemed to be searching for the right words, "but you should know you're welcome any time of the day or night."

"Are you suggesting I sneak out of the cottage in the middle of the night like a horny, love-struck teenager and come to your place?" A surge of excitement rushed through her. The last time she felt this way she'd been in college.

Harmless vacation romance, just to get back on the proverbial dating horse, she assured herself.

This time, he laughed, and when he did, his eyes sparkled, even in the dim light from the truck's dashboard. "I certainly wouldn't turn you away if you did."

"Huh. Well, I'll keep that in mind, sir." Her mind jumped to provisions for the cottage then. They had nothing there. "Hey, you wouldn't mind stopping at a store really quick so I could grab some tea and snacks, would you? We don't have anything at the cottage and I thought some tea and crisps might be handy to have around."

"Of course." With a smile on his face, Sean obliged.

The store didn't take long and they made it home much faster than it had taken to get to Lisdoonvarna, she was sure of it. Of course the ride home always seemed shorter when you wanted the night to continue. He pulled right up to the door of the cottage. It looked as though she was the first one home. Picking up the bag of snacks and tea from the floor board she turned to him.

"Well, I guess this is goodnight." She lifted both of her eyebrows but didn't rush to get out of the truck.

He leaned toward her, pulled her to him, kissing her full on the mouth. His soft lips pressed into hers and her lips parted to taste his tongue. He smelled nice and she loved how his unshaved, rough face scratched her skin. Her body heated up and she dropped the bag to put her arms around him, wanting the kiss to never end.

He pulled away first and she could tell it took a lot of willpower for him to do so. "We shouldn't..."

"No, you're right. Kate or Sarah could get back any minute."

"That's not what I mean." He took a deep breath. "If I don't leave now, I won't. I'll take you inside and that will be the end of that. You're too... beautiful and I want you too badly."

She felt her heart pounding in her chest. She wanted him, too. "I know what you mean, I'd better go then."

He nodded but gave her a reassuring smile.

Once she got to the door, she turned to wave to him before he pulled away and drove back up to the house. The road was awfully dark and if she did sneak out she'd need a flashlight to find her way.

"I can't believe you're actually thinking of doing that," she said aloud to herself. With a laugh and a head shake at her behavior she went inside to calm herself and unpack the bag of tea and snacks before Sarah and Kate got home.

14

Beyond Dusk

When she arrived at the cottage to change it was still early and neither Emily nor Kate were there. Kevin waited patiently and watched some television while she took a shower and changed. A master at fifteen minute showers and five-minute make-up, Sarah ensured they left the cottage by three-thirty. Not because she wanted to avoid Emily and Kate, but because she didn't want to keep Kevin waiting. Her skill at getting ready on-the-fly tended to impress men.

The Gables was a fancy restaurant where the earthy scent of manure and horse sweat wouldn't be welcome. She'd sent the text message declining dinner to their group text thread earlier while she waited for Kevin to get ready.

It wasn't until Sarah and Kevin were in the car heading northeast that her phone chimed.

"OK. I'm having dinner with Sean," Em texted to the group.

Kate responded almost immediately. She sent a frowning emoji with the words. "I'm eating alone?"

"Just tonight," Emily assured her.

Sarah typed a similar message. "For sure dinner tomorrow night."

She cringed when she sent it.

"Your friends not too happy you're having dinner with me?" He seemed upset by that prospect. "Perhaps we should invite them to come with us?"

"No," Sarah said, her response almost too quick. "Emily is having dinner with Sean, the guy we're renting the cottage from. Kate will be fine for a night on her own."

That much was true. Kate had never had issues finding friends wherever she went. She'd undoubtedly find a pub and become the life of the party. Sarah could see Kate now, singing, dancing, and throwing back a few pints. As a crowd loving, independent extrovert, no one ever had to worry about Kate.

"Are you sure?" Kevin didn't sound convinced. "Trust me, Kate is fine with it. She wanted us to have fun on this vacation and we never planned to spend it entirely together anyway." She gave him a forced smile because deep in her gut something told her that Kate was miffed.

She'll get over it, her mind told her. So she put that out of her head and focused on Kevin and dinner. Her stomach growled in response.

The small village of Cleg consisted of a main street with a few shops, a general store with a post office, and that was about it. But there on the corner, according to Kevin, unassuming and quaint, was the best place for scallops for at least fifty miles.

They arrived early enough that it wasn't busy. The hostess showed them to a small table in a back corner and Kevin immediately ordered a bottle of wine and water.

"No beer?" Sarah said after the hostess left, actually relieved that Kevin drank more than just beer. She liked wine more.

He chuckled and picked up the menu. "The scallops. You have to have them, and the risotto. I believe it comes with a steamed vegetable and a salad."

Sarah didn't even pick up the menu. "That sounds perfect."

His eyes narrowed. "Most women wouldn't be so quick to take my suggestion."

"Most women don't have a friend who's a food critic. I learned long ago that if someone else recommends something, try it, because chances are you'll like it. Unless you have completely terrible taste, which I doubt since you're having dinner with me."

The server arrived with a plate of bread and cheese, a bottle of white wine with two wine glasses, and two glasses of water. She set them on the table without any formality and opened the bottle of wine, "Are you ready to order?"

Sarah nodded and Kevin took the liberty of ordering for them both. Once the server was gone, he leaned across the table toward her, his pupils dilated - a sure sign he was into her. "So, as we were discussing earlier, rock climbing…"

She nodded. "I'm just a novice, and I'm kind of afraid of heights, but I have this thing where I have to do things to conquer my fear. With safety straps."

"I might not be that brave. I do snorkel though. I've also been scuba diving."

"I would try both!" The enthusiasm in her voice sounded almost too desperate, so she toned it down. "I swim, but I've never had the opportunity to do either."

"You'd love it. We could go to Belize. The water is so blue you wouldn't believe it." He paused long enough to pour the wine.

She tried to ignore that he just said they could go to Belize, as in *together*. Even though her heart skipped a beat, she kept the conversation on track.

"What about hiking?" Sarah had always been the outdoor type. It was one of the things Eric loved about her.

Their vacations always consisted of outdoor activities whether it was zip-lining, hiking, or horseback riding.

Kevin seemed to share her love of the outdoors, too. "I don't mind going for a hike. There are a lot of places I'd like to hike through."

"There are a lot of places to go hiking where I'm from," she said with a smile. "How do you feel about caves?"

He raised an eyebrow.

She laughed. In college she dated a guy she took on several cave tours. It was when she suggested a third he looked at her and told her in earnest that he hated caves and didn't understand her fascination with dragging him into holes in the ground. Kevin wore a similar expression.

"I don't know how I feel about caves." He shrugged. At least she could rely on hiking and horseback riding.

Wait, she stopped herself. Was she actually considering a serious relationship with Kevin?

"What's wrong? You look like you've just remembered you left the stove on." His hand reached across the table and held hers.

"No, flashback," she lied, pulling her hand away to grab her wine glass. "We should have a toast."

"To?"

"To vacations and spending time in the great outdoors," she told him.

"I'll drink to that." They lifted their glasses in salutation and drank.

Their food arrived rapidly. Or it seemed fast. The scallops were served with an onion butter sauce, and the risotto looked creamy. Broccoli and carrots, steamed of course, garnished the plate.

Sarah paused and looked at the plate, rating the visual appeal.

Now she knew she'd been spending too much time with Kate. "Well," Kevin started, "Are you going to try it?"

Picking up her fork, she skewered a lone scallop and popped it in her mouth. Properly cooked, scallops were tender and delicious, but overcooked they were rubbery and undercooked they were slimy. These were perfect. Closing her eyes she savored the buttery taste and swallowed, nodding. "Yeah, very nice. Fresh."

"They were probably purchased this morning from one of the fish markets," he said, pushing their freshness.

"I bet Kate would love it here." Perhaps suggesting this place would be her penance for leaving Kate to dine on her own tonight.

"If she's into food as much as you say, she shouldn't miss it," Kevin agreed. His attention soon turned to other things. "So what shall we do when we're done here? Go down to the beach and look at the stars? Or we could head back up to my place and find a movie to watch and curl up by the fire?"

The latter sounded fantastic, but now Sarah found herself worried about Kate. Maybe it was best she made it home before nine. Or ten.

"Perhaps a walk on the beach by moonlight, but I really should talk to Kate and Emily. Tomorrow night I'll definitely have to have dinner with them. It wouldn't be right not to," she explained apologetically.

"I understand completely. This is your vacation with your friends and I've been selfish with you." Kevin didn't seem upset in the least. His tone remained mild. "As long as I might be able to spend some additional time with you in the next few weeks. Maybe a few hours here and there? I don't want to get in the way of anything."

"You're not in the way. I want to spend more time with you, too, but I should be spending some time with my friends." She took another scallop and savored it with a mouthful of white wine.

Kevin refilled her glass. "I hope you were a drinker before and I'm not a bad influence."

She laughed. "Oh, I am far from innocent in that department." They spent the remainder of dinner in light-hearted conversation covering favorite colors and foods, as well as favorite vacations. Sarah even told him about she and Eric's horseback riding adventure in the Rocky Mountains and this time she didn't even cry. Not once.

With dinner over, they left Cleg behind them and drove to the road along the coastline, following it to a secluded beach with outcroppings of rock, to look up at the star-filled night sky. They got out of the car. Kevin had a flashlight and a blanket. Here, the light pollution wasn't bad and despite the sliver of a waning moon, they could see the night sky filled with thousands of pinpoints of light. Sarah hadn't seen so many stars since camping at the continental divide. That was the first time she'd ever seen a truly star-filled sky outside a planetarium. Tonight was the second time, and it was beautiful.

Kevin took her hand into his and led her carefully, by flashlight, past the parking area, closer to the water, toward one of the rocks. There, he found a large stone worthy for use as a bench and threw a blanket over it. They sat down close to each other. The cool breeze sent shivers up Sarah's arms. Noticing this, Kevin scooped up the excess blanket behind them, and pulled it up over Sarah's shoulders and put his arm around her. He drew her closer to him.

"Are you warm enough?"

"I'm much better now, thank you." Fighting the urge to rest her head on his shoulder, she looked up to the night sky and let out a wistful sigh. The only sound, aside from her own heart beating in her ears, was the surf pounding on the sand and rocks as the ocean ebbed and flowed.

Just as she was sure she would rest her head on his shoulder and find comfort there, her phone chimed.

Another text message. With a frown she pulled it out of her pocket and looked at it.

"I cut my night short to maybe catch a movie with Kate but she's still out. You coming home soon?" Emily's message asked.

"You need to get back." Kevin stated it plainly as fact. "Yeah, I think Emily is lonely." She let the blanket fall from her shoulders as she stood from the rock.

"All right. I'll have you home in fifteen minutes." They both stood and he scooped up the blanket, using the flashlight to help them pick their way back across the short distance to the car. Kevin opened the car door for her, threw the blanket in the back, and then resumed his position in the driver's seat.

They put on their seat belts and Kevin started toward the cottage. He appeared serene and happy.

"So, you don't often ask women you run into horseback riding back to your place for a drink do you?" The question just kind of popped into her mind and out of her mouth.

"No. You're the first and only," he told her. His answer still left her wanting more.

"What made you think you should ask me back for a drink?"

She narrowed her eyes.

He shrugged. In the darkness she really couldn't make out any expression on his face. "I suppose I felt bad for giving you a fright. You also looked a little lost and in need of company."

"Well thank you for inviting me for that drink," she said, hoping that would smooth over any awkwardness the question dredged up.

"You don't think that you're just a vacation romance do you?

Or one of my many conquests?"

She was caught off guard by his directness. With a sigh she said in a tone as frank as his, "Well, a girl does wonder I guess. I'm just vulnerable right now and I need to know that what I'm experiencing isn't just some rebound romance. I mean, let's be honest. We've only known…"

He cut her off. "Yes. We've only known each other for two days. Have I tried anything dishonorable?"

"No," she admitted.

"I'm not going to. When I told you earlier that I just want us to enjoy one another's company and see where it led, I was serious. I have no desire to push you to anything you're not ready for or take advantage of you." He was quiet as he pulled onto the road leading away from the ocean.

Sarah remained silent until they reached the road leading to the cottage. "I'm sorry. I don't mean to be so paranoid or dramatic. I just need to figure things out. I feel so confused and…" she paused to find just the right word, "Guilty," she finally said.

He pulled into the driveway of the cottage. The car wasn't there and neither was Kate. But the lights were on inside, and she saw Emily pull back the drape and peer out the window.

Kevin turned to her and smiled. "I understand. It doesn't feel right to feel this way about someone else so quickly and so soon. What's a normal grieving period?

What will your friends think? What will your family think? Are you really feeling what you think you're feeling? Or is it all just fleeting? I understand, Sarah. I went through this, too. If I'm nothing else, I'm a patient man. I can be your friend through all of this if you'll just let me. Men and women can be friends, can't they?"

She nodded.

He reached out and gently touched her chin, turning it toward him. "You're putting too much pressure on yourself and worrying too much about defining the nature of our relationship. Don't. Just let happen what happens, and whatever happens you can't judge yourself so harshly. Be kind to yourself. You're still healing. Also remember that I have no intention of taking Eric's place or replacing Gabriella with you. No one can replace either of them."

Compassion filled Kevin's eyes. "But we can find some comfort in each other and perhaps even some healing. All right?"

Sarah forced a smile. "All right."

"Now, promise me you'll stop beating yourself up and go enjoy a night with your friends. When you want to get together again, call me. You have my number."

She laughed. "And how long would it take of me not calling you for you to call me?"

He thought about it briefly. "Forty-eight hours before I have to know if I've been officially de-friended."

Then he took his hand into hers and lifted it to his lips, kissing the back of it. "Have a beautiful night."

Sarah felt herself blush. "Thanks Kevin. Drive home safely."

Getting out of the car, she started toward the door, then turned to watch him drive away. With a big sigh, she went inside to find Emily standing there, anxious to get the scoop.

"So, uh, no goodnight kiss?" she asked with a sly smile. "It's not like that. Kevin and I are just good friends."

"Yes. That scowl on your face says good friends to me." Emily gave her a knowing look. "Sean and I stopped by the store so I could pick up some snacks. Now we just have to wait for Kate. She's allegedly on her way home. I think she was with Aedan."

"If Aedan was working she wasn't. I feel kind of bad leaving her for dinner, but Kevin and I were having so much fun that it seemed natural to want to have dinner..." her voice trailed off.

"Again, as evidenced by that frown. What happened?" Emily started toward the couch and sat down, patting the cushion next to her. "Tell me all about it."

Obediently, Sarah sat down and looked Emily square in the eyes. "I think I'm falling in love with Kevin."

Emily's jaw dropped. "That's big. But it's good, right?"

"No!" Sarah grabbed one of the couch pillows and clutched it with all her might. "No, it's terrible! It's too fast. I'm falling fast and hard and I don't know if I can do this."

Carefully, Emily got up. "You want some tea?"

"I want you to tell me what to do. I'm so confused."

"By the look on your face I see you've already decided."

Em went to the kitchen, leaving Sarah on the couch. "What do you mean?" Sarah continued to frown. "You've already decided to run, and by that I mean you've already got it in your head that you're never going to see Kevin again." A sorrowful look covered Emily's face.

"Yeah," Sarah admitted in defeat. "It's the best thing for both of us. I can't lead him on, and I can't trust myself to keep seeing him. Not to mention there's the small issue of an ocean between us."

Again, Emily didn't answer.

"I know if I keep it up, we're going to end up in bed together and that wouldn't be good for either of us. I mean, I haven't even mourned for a decent amount of time. What kind of woman would Eric think I am if I did that? He'd roll over in his grave. Or come back and haunt me."

This time, Emily's eyes went wide. "Maybe you're being too hasty."

"What?"

"No, hear me out," Emily said. Conservative, mother-hen Emily. "First, how long any person grieves isn't dictated by a specific length of time. You'll always love and miss Eric. Second and more important Sarah, you didn't start crying when you mentioned Eric." Emily started laughing then. "You didn't cry."

Her reaction startled Sarah for a second, but then she realized Emily was right. This evening was probably the first time she hadn't cried at the mention of Eric in five months. "What does that mean?"

"It means you're ready to start living your life again," Emily said as if it was the most obvious thing ever.

A car engine sounded outside signaling Kate was back.

They heard the car door open, then her footfalls on the gravel outside. The door opened and in walked Kate, forcing a smile.

"Sorry I was so late. I was talking to Aedan."

Sarah gave her an apologetic look. "I'm sorry I didn't come back for dinner. I got caught up in the fun and when Kevin asked, I just…"

"Don't worry about it." Kate waved a dismissive hand. Then looked at Emily. "And what about you?"

"By the time Sean and I made it through the castle he thought I might like to have some dinner and I thought it would be rude to say no considering the circumstances. Do you want some tea?" Emily glanced at Sarah, then back at Kate.

Kate seemed to be acting a bit off, like she was hiding something. It didn't last long though. "Okay, I was a bit disappointed because I had a great dinner planned, but we'll just do it tomorrow night."

"Oh good, because the place Sean and I went was good, but not *that* good," Emily admitted, making three cups of tea even though no one had actually said yes about wanting some.

That reminded Sarah to tell Kate about *The Gables*. "Kevin and I went to this really great restaurant in some small town. It's called *The Gables* and the scallops were amazing!"

Kate's face fell. "Well, I guess I'll have to choose something else."

Panic welled in Sarah's stomach. Now she'd done it.

She ruined Kate's dinner plans again without even meaning to. "I would go again so you guys can try it. It was *that good.*"

"Yeah, Sarah doesn't mind eating there again. It's not like she has to have the same thing," Emily said, pouring water from a steaming kettle into the cups.

"All right," agreed Kate.

"So which movie should we watch?" Emily asked.

Sarah knew she was trying to ease the tension and change the subject.

"Maybe a comedy?" she suggested, following Emily's lead. Kate shrugged. "I don't know, I'm feeling kind of tired."

"Oh." Emily gave Sarah a helpless look and Sarah returned it. "Well, tomorrow we should spend the whole day together," she suggested.

With another shrug Kate said, "I had some plans for the morning, but maybe in the afternoon."

"Okay," Sarah agreed.

Emily nodded emphatically. "Do you still want some tea?"

"No, I'm fine. I think I just want to go to bed." Then Kate turned and walked to her room without looking back.

Em carried two of the mugs of steaming tea back to the living room and set them down on the coffee table, then turned to Sarah. "She's pissed at us."

Sarah cringed. "Yeah, I'd say that's a safe bet. And it didn't help that Kevin and I went to that stupid restaurant."

"Don't blame yourself," Emily said. "She'll get glad the same way she got mad."

That was such a mom-thing to say, Sarah thought with a giggle. "Yeah."

"So, movie?"

"It feels wrong to have fun without Kate." She picked up her mug of tea and held its warmth between her hands, finding the heat from the mug comforting.

"Well then I guess we should talk about Kevin," Emily said, turning suddenly serious.

"Actually, I'm more interested in hearing about Sean," Sarah said, turning the tables on her friend. "What's up with that? I thought you thought he was a psycho."

She took a sip of her tea and lifted her eyebrows in question.

Emily wasn't getting out of it that easy.

"Okay, fine," she said, picking up her own tea. "I like Sean and quite frankly, I think I want to sleep with him."

Sarah choked on her tea. "Em!?"

"What? I'm a grown woman, he's a grown man, I like him, he likes me. I haven't had sex with a man in almost two years." Her eyes went to the ceiling as if she were counting. "No, it's been much longer. I can't honestly remember the last time Sam and I had sex before the divorce."

With a dropped jaw, Sarah shook her head. "I can't believe you would just have random sex…"

"It's anything but random. Sometimes when you like a guy you just have to go for it. I mean, just yesterday I thought all guys were jerks and in twenty-four hours, Sean proved me wrong. Did you know he's got a science degree?"

"Did he show them to you?" It was the only question Sarah could get out. She had a million more.

"I don't think he told me that just to impress me if that's what you're saying, but he's not some loser living with his mom. Which brings me to what I wanted to say to you." Again, Emily turned deadly serious. "I think you should go out with Kevin and you shouldn't feel guilty if you have feelings for him. Life is short, Sarah. *Carpe diem*."

Emily lifted her cup and drank.

Biting her inner lip, Sarah followed suit, taking a deep drink of the warm amber liquid in her cup. It had a bitter aftertaste that was somehow satisfying. What were the odds both Emily and Kevin would say the same thing to her in a matter of hours?

Em smiled at her. "You don't want to be one of those women on her death bed wondering what could have been and regretting that you didn't just see something through."

Sarah knew that Emily was talking about herself more than Sarah, but it still held true. Maybe both Emily and Kevin were right. She was over thinking it. What harm could come of just seeing where things went?

15

The Problem with Kate

Kate just got out of the shower when the first text came. It was Sarah saying she was going to have dinner with Kevin. With a sigh, Kate continued to get ready. While she was worried that Sarah was on the rebound, at least she was doing something other than moping around the cottage. That's really what Kate had been worried about.

Everything about Sarah oozed melancholia lately. The vibe she put off permeated the air and brought everyone down under its weight. That's what death did to people who felt deeply.

At least she seemed happy for the moment. It was everything Kate and Emily hoped for. She finished getting dressed and went into the living room to turn on the television. Her phone pinged as another text came through. This time, it was Emily. She was going to dinner with Sean.

"Seriously? You guys are ditching me for guys?" She looked around the empty cottage and shook her head, then texted, "I'm eating alone?"

"Just tonight," came Emily's reply.

"For sure dinner tomorrow night," texted Sarah.

"Fine," Kate said with a heavy sigh. Maybe the whole openness of the vacation hadn't been a good idea. If she had gone to the castle with Emily, then Sean wouldn't have been an issue, but then she wouldn't have been able to spend the day with Aedan. She did have a fun day. Aedan was a nice guy. Cocky, sure, but nice enough. Probably too nice. Too responsible. Of course, *she* wouldn't have ditched her friends to have dinner with him. He could have waited. Sean and Kevin could have waited, too.

"Fine, dinner on my own." With a frown, she wagered her options and decided she didn't feel like going far. It was back to *Mulligan's* for dinner, this time with her laptop in tow just in case she wanted to do some writing. Maybe, if she was lucky, there would be music and friendly people at the pub. She could still have a good time without Sarah and Em. But that didn't change the fact that she was still annoyed.

Mulligan's wasn't as busy tonight. At the last minute, she made a decision to have dinner in the restaurant. Perhaps afterward, she'd go to the pub and enjoy a beer. Even as she thought it, she felt lonely. Her heart wasn't in it. Sure, she could usually have fun anywhere she went. Men tripped over themselves to buy her drinks and talk to her. She was the life of the party, but tonight she just wasn't in the mood. Her carefully laid out plans had been altered.

Tonight, no one seemed overly friendly toward her.

Even the waitress seemed a bit stand-offish. Maybe it was the moon.

Usually, she had fun picking out what she was going to eat, but the menu looked bland and common. After fifteen minutes she decided on the duck. Not a lot of chefs could prepare duck to her liking. Aedan could. Instead of alcohol, she chose tea to accompany her meal, and once the waitress had left with her order, she pulled out her laptop and began working on the first of her articles.

She didn't notice him pull out a chair and sit down. "So what happened to *The Gables*?"

Pausing from typing, she looked up to see Aedan's green eyes peering at her with concern.

"It seems Sarah and Emily had other plans. Shouldn't you be cooking?"

"You seem upset."

"No, it gives me time to work. I was worried about when I'd have time to write these articles, but it seems I had nothing to worry about."

"You are upset." He cringed. "Is there anything I can do?"

"Well, you can show me again how well you can prepare

duck." She stopped herself, realizing how rude that was. "I'm sorry. I'm not usually a horrible, rude person."

"Just with me?"

Tipping her head and letting out a sigh she made another

attempt at an apology. "It's a defense mechanism. I am truly sorry. When my needs aren't being met, I tend to lose my cool."

"I am no stranger to women with a little fire. I dated a ginger for a year. She was mostly psychotic..."

Kate laughed.

Aedan smiled, obviously happy that he was able to lighten the mood. "I'm sure your friends think that they see you all the time. It's not often they get to see Ireland escorted by a local."

She snorted and didn't care how undignified it sounded. "You and I both know it's all about vacation romance and no-strings- attached sex."

He let out a laugh. "Is it now?"

"What are the odds both of my friends, who don't date back home, would meet two awesome guys and actually fall in love?" The entire idea was preposterous. "I'm sure you guys enjoy all the tourists ready to fall into the arms of the first Irish man they come across who sweet-talks them."

"Wow. That's rather insulting," Aedan said, no longer amused. "Why are you insulted? I didn't mean you. You haven't put the

moves on me and even if you did, I wouldn't blow off my friends to swoon over you."

His tone turned defensive. "While I admit that I don't know Kevin MacClery much at all, I do know Sean O'Flannigan, and I know he's not the type to lure vacationers into his bed. He's probably just being hospitable and if he does like your friend, then he genuinely likes her."

"Well, we'll see." The frown remained on her face.

"I suppose I should get back to the kitchen, but in the meantime," he stopped when the waitress brought the tea by and waited until she left, "stop frowning. You're scaring people."

Her jaw dropped. Did he really just say that? "I'm cute when I frown."

"No, you're scary when you frown, and when you're cranky you're kind of a bitch." With that, Aedan O'Byrne stood up, turned and went back to his kitchen, leaving Kate staring after him in shock.

It took her a few minutes to recover. Her mind started racing with possible hidden meanings. Was he upset? Was he being a smart ass? Or was he just being a guy and saying exactly what he meant at that moment? *No, it doesn't matter what he thinks of you,* she told herself. Then she thought, *however, if you have to tell yourself it doesn't matter, it does. Why does it matter?*

With a sigh, she resolved to stay and, at least, finish dinner, and then she'd go around to the pub for a pint and try to make the best of an evening gone to crap.

When dinner came, she looked toward the kitchen, hoping to see Aedan there, but he didn't come out. She ate slowly, not because she wanted to savor it, but because her own melancholy prevented her from enjoying it. Truthfully it was probably some of the best duck she'd ever had. It was already dark out by the time she finished.

The pub was dark, full of people, and a woman playing a harp sat on the small stage in the back. Her hands glided over the strings, producing sad notes that hung thick in the air. It was enough to make Kate feel like she wanted to hurl herself from a cliff. She felt ready to when a hand touched her shoulder.

"Drinking alone doesn't suit you." It was Aedan. He sat down next to her.

Her heart skipped a beat.

Minding her tone, she forced a smile. "I'm not alone. I'm here, in a pub, surrounded by thirty people, give or take."

"Look, I'm sorry for saying what I said, but…" She let out an audible, forlorn sigh and cut him off.

"But I'm a cranky bitch. Is this one of those sorry, not sorry kind of apologies? Because if it is - just own what you said. I deserved it. You're right."

She looked down at her hands and started picking at a cuticle.

His eyes followed hers.

"I just don't think your reactions or conclusions are always reasonable or kind." He grabbed her beer and took a drink.

She couldn't help but smile and point to her beer in his hand. "You keep doing that. It's annoying."

Aedan started laughing and set her beer back down. "But it got you to smile."

He was right, she was definitely smiling now.

"I thought you were angry with me. Like, never-want-to- speak-to-me-again angry," she admitted, watching his facial expression.

"I would never not want to speak to you," he said, then put his hand into hers. "But I wish you'd be more trusting and find the good in people. I also hope you'll be more forgiving of a bad piece of meat in the stew next time, because we both know there will be another next-time."

His touch comforted her and made her feel welcome again. It was nice to have a friend. Of course, it didn't change the fact that she was still disappointed with Sarah and Em. Em more than Sarah. Sarah still got a free pass, at least for another six months, while she grieved.

Maybe she was being stupid and petty. Finally, she said, "Thanks, Aedan."

"I'll tell you what, next time your friends decide to leave you on your own for dinner, let me know. I'll leave early, or I'll get one of the guys to cover me for the night. That way you won't have to eat alone."

A weak smile surfaced. "Oh, I don't mind eating alone..."

"Don't be stubborn," he told her. "Now I have to go back to

work because I still have a few hours left, but I want you to, at least, try my chocolate cake before you go."

"Chocolate cake?"

"It's comfort food and you look like you could use a piece." He got up and patted her shoulder. "I'll be right back with it."

"I think that Aedan is sweet on you," said an older woman at the next table.

Kate turned her weak smile on the stocky brunette. "We're just friends."

"Always best to start as friends," the woman said, then turned her attention back to the haunting music ebbing forth from the woman playing the harp.

Aedan returned a minute later with a plate of cake and set it in front of her. "Now I won't take no for an answer. You eat this, go home, take a warm bath and get into bed and I guarantee you'll feel better in the morning."

She chuckled.

"It's already working, ain't it now?" He winked at the stocky brunette.

The woman laughed. "That's our Aedan. Cooking and bakin' his way into women's hearts."

Then Aedan gave Kate one last knowing look before returning to his kitchen for the rest of the night.

She finished the cake, eating it slowly as she did dinner, but this time not because she was upset. Instead, she wanted to savor every sweet, velvety bite.

On the way home, she rehearsed what she wanted to say to Sarah and Emily. She wanted to tell them that she felt abandoned and lonely and brushed off in favor of people they'd just met.

When she opened the door to the cottage and found them both in the living room. She put on the biggest smile she could manage and completely lost her nerve. "Sorry I was so late. I was talking to Aedan."

Sarah gave her a guilty look and an excuse. Emily did the same. Kate pretended it was no big deal, even though she felt abandoned by her best friends. She found herself saying, "Okay, I was a bit disappointed because I had a great dinner planned, but we'll just do it tomorrow night."

That's when Emily dropped the bomb. She'd already been to *The Gables*. Now Kate couldn't take them there tomorrow night and she'd have to find another place.

The rest of the conversation was a blur. Emily insisted she could eat there again, Kate agreed, then she felt sick to her stomach. She just wanted to go to bed. Maybe Aedan sensed it and knew how she was feeling. He had suggested she come home, take a warm bath and go to bed.

Emily suggested they spend the day together, but Kate wasn't sure she wanted to because now it felt obligatory. Like her friends *knew* they'd ditched her and now they were trying to make up for it. They didn't truly want to spend the time together.

"I had some plans for the morning, but maybe in the afternoon," she lied.

Somewhere in that conversation, she was sure she had said she was disappointed about being left on her own, but she didn't remember because going to her room was a blur and when she shut the bedroom door all she wanted to do was crawl into bed and stay there. That's exactly what she did.

The alarm went off at eight the following morning.

Kate's first thought was to wonder if she was the one being the jerk. If she wasn't, didn't her friends owe her an apology? Or at least some sincerity in their alleged want to spend time with her? As she got up and showered, she could feel the mood for the entire day set in and decided quickly that she needed to get out of the cottage before anyone woke up.

It worked. She found herself in the car and heading toward the ocean before anyone knew she was gone. She'd find a nice place on the beach to go for a walk to clear her head. It seemed no matter what she did, nothing was working.

She spent the entire gray, cold morning walking up and down the beach with her hands shoved deep in her jacket pockets, dwelling on why she was mad. Knowing it wasn't doing her any good, she decided to go home. The only way to resolve the issue was to go back to the cottage and confront it head on.

When she got there, she found Sarah and Emily were there. She half expected they'd be long gone, having given up on her and gone off to do something more interesting than wait for Kate to come around.

She walked in the door pretending everything was normal, but she knew it wasn't and so did Emily and Sarah.

"All right, let's talk," Emily started in that annoying, motherly tone.

So what if Emily was older? Kate wasn't a child. "About?" Sarah groaned.

Emily kept her cool. "About why you're pissed at us." Kate felt her jaw stiffen. "Fine. I'm angry with you both."

"Because?"

"Are you trying to head-shrink me?"

Shaking her head, Emily said, "No, Kate. I want us to work this out. What's going on?"

"You really don't get it, do you? I spend months putting together a great vacation. I spend hours laboring over finding these great restaurants to try. I tried my best to make sure we spend some time together and the first two guys who show any interest in getting in your pants, and your both off like wildfire and it's see ya Kate! You're on your own!" She didn't bother sitting or taking her purse off her shoulder.

"Well, you've pretty much stranded us both here without cars, so we are at the mercy of locals to drive us places. I only went with Sean last night because he asked and I figured having dinner with him was the least I could do. Turning him down seemed rude. Especially since I took him away from his work to go visit a castle I wanted to see."

"I told you I would have gone to the castle with you," Kate spat.

"Really? You would have been bored out of your mind. You like to shop and check out social scenes, I want to sight- see," Emily countered.

"You could have at least told Sean another time, *Kate is home waiting for me*, or, at least, invited him along."

Emily didn't respond, but Sarah finally chimed in. "It was one night, Kate. If we knew you felt this strongly about it, we would have come home last night."

"And you - what the hell do you think you're doing rebounding with some wealthy Irish playboy?" It just came out. Kate couldn't stop it. She was worried about Sarah being used by some guy to get his jollies.

Sarah's jaw dropped and Emily stood up.

"Now hold on. Let's stop with the accusations… this is ridiculous. We shouldn't be fighting."

"Stop with the passive aggressive crap okay? Why am I the only one not allowed to have an opinion or feelings about something?" This sent Kate off in an entirely new tirade, one she hadn't explored in her head yet. "Am I not allowed to feel excluded and casually tossed aside in favor of some guys you both just met? What the hell am I supposed to think?"

She paused long enough to consider her next words. "Aedan thought I was being rude and insulting when I suggested these guys are just using you both for a fun time, but I think it was because I'm right. Do you know what Europeans in general think of American women? They think we're easy. That's why they naturally come to us looking for sexual flings when we visit their countries."

"Yeah, I agree with Aedan, that's pretty rude and insulting," Emily agreed then said, "Do you really think that's how Sean is?"

Kate frowned. "I don't know because I don't know him. And neither do you! I'm just wondering what hold these men have over you two that you would ditch me!"

"For crying out loud, Kate! Do you hear yourself? We said we were sorry! We said we'd be more sensitive in the future - what more do you want?" The tea kettle went off and Emily stomped into the kitchenette.

"You want us to be miserable," Sarah said with a sullen expression.

Kate couldn't believe her ears. "What?"

"You have tailored this entire trip around saving me from myself. Well damn it, Kate, I'm a grown woman and if I want to spend all my time with, or even *fuck* some Irish playboy, then that's what I'm going to do. Maybe I am on the rebound and maybe he is using me, but you know what?" Sarah teared up and before too long, the torrent of tears flowing down her cheeks. "Maybe for the past couple of days I've been having fun. Laughing and enjoying my life. For the first time since Eric died, I can finally see a future for myself. I'm sorry if you can't handle that and it hurts your feelings. I didn't mean to hurt your feelings or upset you by having fun and not weighing my every decision on how it would make *you* feel. Maybe that was insensitive of me, but I didn't mean to snub you, and I will NOT sit here and listen to you feel sorry for yourself and try to ruin what little happiness I have right now because you had to have dinner by yourself for one damn night!"

Sarah got up from the couch and stomped from the room, slamming her bedroom door behind her.

Kate and Emily were left staring at each other.

But then Emily set down the kettle and quietly left the room, probably to check on Sarah.

Kate didn't stick around. She went straight to the pub.

16

Drowning Her Sorrows

The pub wasn't that busy, so Kate made her way straight to the bar and sat down.

"What'll you have?" asked the bartender.

Without skipping a beat, she said, "A double shot of whatever cheap whiskey you have, and a Guinness, please."

Right now she felt like an ass. She knew she was being petty the minute Sarah flipped out. Sarah was right. Kate did want her friends to be happy because of her and it did piss her off that they wanted to spend time with strangers instead of her. If that made her selfish, then she was most definitely being selfish. She just wasn't sure how to stop being that way.

Warily, the bartender set the whiskey in front of her and went to get her beer. He kept glancing over at her and shaking his head.

She didn't care. She downed the whiskey in a few mouthfuls, barely containing her want to gag. Whiskey was awful, but it was a quick way to numb how horrible she felt.

Setting the empty glass on the bar, she motioned for the bartender to give her another.

Shaking his head, he filled the glass again.

In one swig, she tossed it down the back of her throat. "More?" he asked, still holding the bottle.

"One more."

"That's a lot of whiskey for a woman your size."

"One more," she repeated, then added, "Please." He filled the glass a third time.

This time, she just took a mouthful. The horrific taste was as good as any punishment she could have given herself. A few minutes later the bartender returned, this time with her beer. "Here you are."

"Thank you."

He shook his head again and went to help someone at the far side of the bar.

After she finished the third whiskey and half the beer her inhibitions were completely obliterated and her body felt numb and malleable.

She saw the bartender say something to a server, who immediately disappeared, then he approached her.

"Another?" He nodded toward the now empty glass of whiskey.

She nodded at him, took out her credit card, and set it down on the bar.

He took the card and the glass, and returned with a full glass and the card. "I started a tab. When you're done, you can sign for it."

With a quick nod, she grabbed the card and dropped it onto the floor.

Aedan O'Byrne picked it up. "You've gone and gotten yourself drunk."

It wasn't a question or accusation. Just a statement of fact. "I take it your confrontation with your friends didn't go

well." He set the card back up on the bar.

This time, she managed to pick it up and secure it back in her wallet, and put it in her purse without incident, but it took strong concentration to manage it. "Sarah is a bitch," she slurred.

Then she thought better of what she said. "No, I is the bitch."

Aedan laughed.

"It's not funny that I'm a bitch. Tell me Aedan..." She said *Aedan* without pronouncing the second *a*. "Do you think I'm a terrible person? You said I was a bitch."

He sighed. "We can all be nasty if we want to be. I can see why you were upset with your friends, but you couldn't see it until now. Now you go about correcting yourself."

"How am I gonna do that?" She downed the fourth glass of whiskey, set the glass on the table, and then grabbed the beer.

"First, I'm cutting you off." With the wave of his hand, he had the bartender clear the whiskey glass from in front of her. "No more of that and no more beer after this one."

"You can't cut me off, I'm a grown woman." Whether or not what came out of her mouth sounded like that was another story. The room spun for a second, but she stopped it by setting her right foot on the ground. Then she slammed the rest of the beer.

Aedan literally took the beer glass out of her hand and handed it to the guy behind the bar. "No, you're done. As a worker at this establishment, I'm cutting you off for your own safety. And the safety of others."

She became vaguely aware of other bar patrons watching her. "What the hell?"

"Come on," Aedan helped her off the stool, paused long enough so she could sign for her drinks. Then, with his arm around her he helped her outside. "Where are your keys?"

Reaching into her pocket, she produced them along with some pocket lint. She laughed and handed him the keys.

"I'm taking you home."

"You can't take me home, I'm not going back to those bitches, because I'm a horrible person." She balked and pulled away from him.

"Fine, I'll take you back to my place. You can sleep on the couch." He was far stronger than her and easily wrestled her into her car's passenger seat and buckled her in while passers- by looked on, entertained by the scene.

Aedan forced a smile and gave them a polite hello, then got into the driver's seat.

"Don't you have to work?" Kate was suddenly concerned for his job.

"I'm off tonight, but I can't have a drunk woman disrupting the place, and as my friend, I couldn't just kick you onto the street to pass out in a gutter. You'd end up in jail to sober up." He shook his head.

They drove for what seemed like forever and she felt like her body was being tossed around like a rag doll. The car finally stopped and Aedan got out. After unbuckling her, he carefully hoisted her from the seat and got her to her feet.

Her stomach lurched and she fell forward onto her knees, throwing up the contents of her stomach onto the gravel driveway.

She felt his hands pull her hair back while he waited for her to finish.

"Let that be a lesson on what four glasses of whiskey will do to you." Then he lifted her again and her legs gave way beneath her.

He readjusted and picked her up, carrying her up some steps and into the house. When he set her on the couch, she immediately melted into it.

"I'll bring you a trash bin and some water just in case you get sick again." He disappeared long enough that she fell asleep. When he returned, she woke up briefly. Long enough to see the trash can and the water, and to feel him wiping her face with a cool, wet rag. "Sleep well, Kate

Berkhill. That's one hell of a hangover you'll have once you sober up," he said.

She felt him pull a light blanket over her. That was all she remembered from the day before.

Waking to bright light, a dog barking, and a ringing phone when your head is throbbing in pain is not the way to start the morning. She grabbed her head and howled. "Damn it! How long have I been sleeping?"

Sitting up, she squinted at the light, realizing it was just the sun coming in the front window and streaming right into the room she was in. Aedan's place wasn't overly tidy. It was cluttered. On a table, next to the couch sat the water from the night before. She looked down at herself, thankful she hadn't thrown up again.

A big yellow dog stood at the screen door looking out, barking. A cool breeze filled the house. She heard a man's footfalls from somewhere behind the couch.

"Maggie, knock it off. It's a bird, you silly git." He set down a bottle of pills next to the water near her head and it sounded like he slammed them down. "You just slept away fifteen hours of your life."

"Ugh."

"Told you that would be one hell of a hangover. What possessed you to do that?"

She held up a hand to stop him. "I don't need a lecture. I know, I'm a complete idiot."

Her hand went back to her head as if cupping her temples would somehow stop the pain.

"Well, take the ibuprofen. It should help."

The dog, a yellow lab now that she could see more clearly, started barking again.

"Mags, stop-it." Aedan went back into a room off the living room. She heard him rustling pots and pans around. Then she smelled frying bacon. Her stomach growled.

No wonder she'd gotten so drunk and sick. She hadn't eaten dinner. The dog looked at her from the door and wagged its tail.

"Hey, Maggie," she said. The mere utterance of the dog's name made it pad over to her gleefully and stick her muzzle right in Kate's lap. She pet Maggie. "Okay, doggy. I need to take something for this headache."

With a mouthful of water, she downed two of the ibuprofens. Her stomach growled and she realized she better chase it down with some food or she'd be nauseated again before too long. Her eyes searched for signs of a bathroom.

"Where is your lavatory?" She normally would have said toilet, but for some reason, that seemed too crude to say around Aedan.

"Down the hallway, first door on the left. Breakfast should be ready soon." His voice echoed from the kitchen, but he didn't come out.

She made her way around the couch and down the hall, still feeling a bit unsteady on her feet. The mirror in the bathroom didn't lie. Kate looked terrible. Without any makeup or fresh clothes, she'd have to make do. She rinsed her face and combed her hair, then straightened her clothes. Luckily she had some perfume with her, so she gave herself a spritz. She'd have to have a proper shower when she got back to the cottage. That was not what she was looking forward to.

When she emerged from the bathroom, she found Maggie waiting for her, tail wagging. She gave the dog a pat and made her way to the kitchen.

There, Aedan was just putting breakfast onto plates. Nothing fancy, just eggs with onion and peppers, sausage, bacon and toast. Her stomach growled audibly.

"I figured you better eat something. Drinking on an empty stomach is one thing, a hangover on an empty stomach is another."

She nodded in agreement. "I can't believe I did that. What's wrong with me?"

Flopping down in the chair, a gray tabby cat jumped into the chair next to her. Aedan grabbed two bowls from the counter and put dog food in one and cat food in the other, then set them down in separate corners. The dog and the cat followed to their own bowls and began eating.

"Can't forget the rest of the family."

"No eggs, bacon and sausage for them?"

He rinsed his hands and then dried them off. "Sometimes, but not when onions are involved or company is here. You want some tea?"

"Okay." Tea sounded fine, but coffee would have been better. She decided to keep that to herself. It was kind enough of Aedan to let her stay with him for a night, let alone make her breakfast.

First he set the tea in front of her, then the plate of food with a fork. Only then did he grab his own tea and breakfast and join her at the table.

"Thank you, Aedan. I feel like such a jerk." She managed a weak smile before taking a bite of eggs. It was so good she didn't realize how quickly she was eating.

"Well, I'm glad you came to your senses, but what were you thinking, drinking like that?" He wasn't going to drop it.

"I figured I could drown my sorrows and things would magically fix themselves. But we both know it doesn't work that way." She paused to take a long drink of the strong tea. "I wasn't finished feeling sorry for myself."

"Are you done now?" A smile played on his lips. Evidently he found her amusing.

"Maybe. We'll see. Now I need to figure out how to make everything right again and I don't know how I'm going to do it."

"Well, you could just apologize and tell your friends you were wrong," he suggested as if it was the easiest thing in the world.

"That will probably work with Em, but I'm not so sure it would work with Sarah. She was right in everything she said. She said I was trying to save her, and was upset that it was a guy who made her happy and not me, or this trip.

She's right. I am totally jealous of her friend. I said some bad things." She frowned.

Aedan lifted an eyebrow and tipped his head to one side.

"You told her he was using her for sex?"

"You're psychic?"

"No, I just have a keen insight into people and you told me you didn't think the guy was on the level. You insinuated any men who were nice to you while you were here were just looking for sex. You're entirely too jaded, Kate. I think you need to start dating men who aren't so..." He paused to pick the right word. "Childish. Boorish. Man-whores. You deserve better than that."

Her frown deepened as she remembered back to her sister and Josh. Aedan was right. They were both whores - her sister, and Josh.

"We all behave badly when our own needs aren't being met, or we're fearful of something. It's human nature," he said.

She chewed thoughtfully on a piece of bacon. "I just don't know how I'm going to apologize yet. She's really into *this guy*."

"There you go again. *This guy*. He has a name, doesn't he?" Aedan took a bite of his own breakfast.

Kate started on her toast, but waited to swallow the bite in her mouth before speaking. "Yeah, Kevin I think."

Aedan laughed. "That's a start. Start by calling him Kevin."

"Well that's hardly going to fix everything, is it?"

"No, but it's a start to respecting your friend's feelings.

Next, give her enough credit for being smart enough to make her own decisions. Her fiancé may have died, but she's not a child. People grieve in their own time. I knew a man who married again ten months after his wife passed on. She wouldn't have wanted him wallowing in sorrow forever. His kids weren't happy about it, but they grew to accept it. Sarah is still young. Perhaps she's grieved long enough."

"I'm just worried she's going to get hurt." She sighed.

"I know." He reached over and took her empty tea cup and went to get her another cup. "In time I think she'll realize you were only trying to keep her from getting hurt, too, but you can't protect her from everything forever.

She's lived through the death of someone she loves. I think she can handle another relationship. Even if it doesn't develop into anything more than a dalliance."

Kate realized then that Aedan was right. Sarah wasn't some delicate flower to be handled with kid gloves. As a matter of fact, she could recall quite a few times where Sarah was the strong one. When Emily had first announced her divorce, it was Sarah who helped her find the lawyer and gave Emily the courage to go through with it. Not Kate. Oh sure, Kate was the one in the cheerleading section for support, but she'd never been the one Emily leaned on. Now, it was Emily who had been strong for Sarah. Again, Kate was only the support staff, planning a trip to make it all better again. Like applying a bandage or kissing a boo-boo.

"I guess it's time for me to suck it up and do whatever it takes to make things right. I still want to salvage the trip. Make it so we can still have fun. We still have a couple of weeks. It feels like we've been here for months already." She forced a weak smile.

He set another cup of tea in front of her and squeezed her shoulder. "It will be fine. Now, since you still have a few weeks, we should talk about you and me going into Galway to check out a new restaurant. It's called *Briarwood* and I know the chef from cooking school. I'd like to check it out, and it would be a perfect place for you to review since it's trendy."

"What about Sarah and Em?"

"I'm sure they'll find other things to do." He smiled at her. "How about it? Do I have a dinner date? Or will I have to go alone, or take Sean? He cleans up well, but he's the type who thinks pub food is fancy and everything tastes good. I can say that since he's my friend."

This time, she laughed. "You're saying you need a more refined dinner date?"

"I do. I'm curious to know whose cooking is better. Mine or my old chum from cooking school." He smiled and took a bite of toast.

"Ah, so that's what this is about. You need some chef ego stroking?" Holding back a laugh she gave him a coy smile. Her headache seemed to be subsiding. The food in her stomach combined with the ibuprofen seemed to be working.

"Absolutely. I have a fragile chef's ego and I want my friends to think I'm the best cook they've ever known."

"I think I would like to find out if that's the case," she agreed.

"Excellent. Just give me a few days' notice after you check with your friends, so I can make a reservation."

"How am I going to get home?"

"We brought your car here, remember?" She didn't.

"I thought you could drop me back off at the pub so I can get my car, then you could head back to the cottage, if that's okay with you," he suggested. Aedan's green eyes sparkled. He hadn't shaved yet this morning, so the blond bed-head coupled with five o'clock shadow made him more handsome than ever. He wore shorts and a t-shirt. His legs looked to be pure muscle. She began to wonder what his abs looked like, but quickly stopped herself. They were just friends.

"We can do that." She took another sip of tea and tried to focus on finishing breakfast.

Just like Aedan suggested, she took him to his car, then headed back to the cottage nervous as hell. Butterflies danced in her stomach and she felt queasy. While nothing felt nearly as awful as being at odds with her best friends, knowing she would have to eat crow wasn't much better.

Her own stupidity and selfishness humiliated her. In her head, she rehearsed the things she'd say to make it right. "I'm sorry for being so selfish and ignorant of what you're going through and I didn't mean any of those things I said," seemed perfect for Sarah while, "I'm a terrible friend and I'm selfish and horrible," was the plan for Emily. Even as she thought these words and how she would say them, tears welled up in her eyes. It was going to be a rough morning.

When she arrived at the cottage, it looked desolate and barren on the outside. The drapes were still drawn and it was silent within. She entered cautiously, feeling hopeless.

Emily had her back facing the door when Kate entered. She seemed focused on the mug of tea in front of her. Kate cleared her throat and closed the door behind her.

Emily turned around and saw her. "You didn't stay here last night." Her voice sounded nervous.

"No. I stayed with Aedan."

Her friend's eyes went wide. "You slept with Aedan?"

"No. I spent the night on the couch. I had a little too much to drink." Kate sighed. "Look, Em, I'm sorry I was such a selfish jerk last night. I had no business saying anything I said. I feel awful and I don't want us to fight."

Emily didn't acknowledge her right away. She appeared to be distracted, her eyes staring off into the distance. "That's all right, Kate. I was over it last night. I have a bigger problem."

"What happened?"

"I slept with Sean." The words hung thick in the air. "I mean, I knew I wanted to and then we did, and before he woke up this morning, I left and came back here and now I feel terrible for leaving."

Kate dropped her bag on the table and sat down on the couch. Emily joined her. "I'm sure he'd understand."

"That I used him and then left?" A forlorn sigh escaped her lips. "I just can't face him today."

She wasn't sure what to say and she didn't want to presume anything or make a comment that might further the damage she'd already done. "I understand," was all she said.

"What am I going to do?" Emily pressed.

"You should, at least, talk to him. Or maybe you could just say you got a text from me and came home so we could talk?" she suggested. The scent of flowers seemed to fill the room and Kate looked over at the air freshener. The breeze must have caught it just right and caused a flood of fragrance.

Emily's eyes lit up. "That would certainly save face and not make me look like a complete jackass. I hate lying to him, though."

"Do you regret it?" Deep down, Kate winced, hoping the question didn't sound judgmental. After all, it's not like she was chaste and virginal. She had been known to jump into bed with a guy after the first few dates.

"No, I just feel bad because I feel like I'm just using him for sex. Which is kind of embarrassing. I'm not that type of girl," Em said as if she was trying to convince Kate.

Kate knew Emily well enough to know that wasn't the case. "But he's a grown man, surely he could have said no if he wasn't interested."

"True." Emily smiled. "Do you want some tea?"

"Sure." Emily's phone rang. "It's Sarah."

Good, Kate thought. Sarah was the one she really needed

to apologize to.

"Hello," Emily said, her voice more cheerful now. Then the smile on her face faded to a look of sheer horror. "Oh my God. What happened?"

The fine hairs on Kate's arms stood straight on end. Whatever happened, it wasn't good.

17

Kevin's Comfort

"I need to get out of here." Sarah pushed past Emily and pulled out her suitcase. She began packing.

"Where are you going?"

"I'm going to stay with Kevin and see if he'll give me a ride to the airport when it's time."

Emily winced. "Please don't go."

She whirled around with a handful of shirts clutched in her fist. "I can't stay here with her Em! She's driving me crazy. When we first got here, she wouldn't let me out of her sight, and now she doesn't want either of us to have any fun. Notice how not once she mentioned how she's been all about Aedan since we got here."

"But what about me? What am I going to do?"

With a sniff, Sarah shoved her remaining belongings into her suitcase and zippered it shut. It appeared she hadn't fully unpacked anyway. "If I stick around here I might just disappoint you, too. Because, Em, while I love you, and Kate, I just need a break from my life and from Kate."

Emily's eyes welled up with tears and Sarah dropped her bag, embracing her friend. "I'll see you on the plane on the way home." With that, Sarah grabbed her suitcase and went past Emily, walking straight out of the cottage. She didn't bother to stop and call Kevin, she decided she'd start walking toward the main road

and he could pick her up.

He answered on the second ring. "Sarah. I wasn't expecting to hear from you. I'm glad you called though."

"Kevin," she interrupted, "Did you mean what you said when you said I could stay with you?"

"Of course. What happened?" His voice turned dead serious.

She ignored his question. "Could you come get me? I'm heading out to the main road now. I need a place to stay for a couple of weeks."

"I'll be right over. Give me fifteen minutes. Maybe ten." Then the phone on the other end went dead and she put her cell phone away, continuing up the hill and past the O'Flannigan house. Like usual, Mrs. O'Flannigan was outside sweeping the porch, like she always seemed to be when someone was going by.

"Are you leaving?" the woman asked.

Sarah stopped walking and switched her suitcase to the other hand. It was kind of heavy.

"I'm going to spend the rest of my time here with a friend," Sarah explained, wiping her eyes.

She must have looked awful because the women appeared concerned and frowned. "Oh my dear, you and your friends have had an argument."

Sarah nodded. "Just with Kate. Emily is okay."

Why was she telling this woman, a complete stranger, all of this?

"Would you like to come in for a cup of tea?" Mrs. O'Flannigan's look of concern and the empathy in her voice were both genuine.

"No, Kevin will be here soon. Thank you though." She forced a warm smile and started walking again and the older woman watched after her as she went.

Sarah could feel the eyes on her back and once she got over the hill and started down toward the main road, she could breathe a little easier.

Kevin pulled up alongside her after she'd been walking down a stretch of road with fields on either side for about five minutes. "Here, let me get that."

He started to get out of the car, but Sarah motioned him back in and climbed right into the passenger side, shoving her suitcase in the back. "Don't bother. No need to be formal, especially when I look like this."

Kevin didn't say anything. He just looked at her until she fastened her seatbelt, then pulled back onto the empty road.

Sarah was the one to finally break the silence. "I always knew Kate could be selfish, but after all, she did for me when Eric died, I guess I kind of forgot. I had no idea she didn't want me to be happy."

He kept his eyes on the road and didn't say anything, which was fine with her. Right now she just needed someone to listen.

"I mean, I just can't stand being in the same house with her. She accused you of being some jerk who was just using me for sex, as if you prey on unsuspecting American women all the time." A sigh escaped her lips.

This time, Kevin said something. "Well, you know my secret now. I randomly ride up on strangers, scare their horses, and invite them to my lair of debauchery. Then I seduce them with my alluring accent, and finally, I whisk them away to my bed chamber and steal their common sense with a kiss."

A wide grin covered his lips.

Sarah rolled her eyes and smiled. "Yes, as if I'm some easily led girl who doesn't know any better. And even if you were just trying to seduce me, if I said yes, then it was consensual and maybe I wanted to be seduced. Right?"

"So that's what it's about huh? She's being overprotective of you again."

Kevin's comment made her pause. "Yeah, I guess so.

It's like I can only be happy if it's on Kate's terms. She wanted to be the reason for my happiness. She never suspected it would be a guy I just met."

"Wait, I make you happy?" He smiled and bit his lower lip. "Yes, you do make me happy," she admitted, hoping it wouldn't go to his head.

"I suppose I can see where that might make her a bit jealous." He turned on the road leading up to his house. "She spends months trying to bring you around, but can't accept that maybe you just needed to be able to talk to someone who has been where you are."

Sarah nodded, feeling more tears coming. She was so tired of tears. Some days it felt like she had nothing left to cry.

"Sorry, I shouldn't be saying anything. I should just be listening." They pulled up the driveway and he stopped the car directly across from the front door of the manor house.

Sarah regained her composure. "No, it's okay. It's good to get feedback."

"I'll carry the case." He reached into the back and grabbed her suitcase.

She didn't protest and followed him into the house. He started up the stairs. "I am going to put you in the Rose Suite. It's not near my room, so if you need anything in the middle of the night you'll have to yell for me, but it does have an incredible view, its own washroom, and it's quiet. It will give you some privacy," Kevin said.

Kevin was always the gentleman and for that, Sarah was thankful. If Kate was right and she was being seduced, she couldn't tell. A man who wanted to seduce a woman didn't usually put her in the room furthest from his own. Nor was a desperate man respectful of her space or privacy.

When they reached the top of the stairs, he pointed to the right. "My room is all the way to the right of the stairs, yours will be all the way to the left."

He led her to the left and they walked to the end of the hall, to a brass handled door. Opening it, he went inside and set the case down on a luggage table. Then he went to one of the windows and opened the drapes, revealing a large sized room with its own closet, phone and television. Opposite the bed, a large bathroom.

"I will have the housekeeper get you fresh towels," he said, opening another drape. "And here's that view I promised."

She came up alongside him at the window and looked out, down onto the forest and green hills below. In one of the fields, she saw two riders on horseback. That must have been the trail she was on the day she first met Kevin. She remembered looking up at the houses on the ridge as she rode past, thinking rich people must live up here. Never did she imagine that a few days later she'd be staying in one of those houses looking down at the valley below.

Kevin sat quietly, waiting for her to respond to the view. "This is perfect."

"Well, how about I leave you to settle in and get comfortable.

Feel free to wander around the house, find a book in the library or watch television. Whatever you like. We can go for a ride later if you're up for it." He started toward the door, kind of lingering just inside.

"Thanks, Kevin," she said after him.

He smiled and politely left, pulling the door closed behind him and leaving her alone.

Sarah spent about ten more minutes looking out the window at the riders and horses below, watching their tiny figures move along the trail until they disappeared into the forest. They looked so small from up here.

Now she had to decide what to do. Did she take a shower then a nap? Should she unpack and walk around the house? She was kind of hungry. Would it be presumptuous to help herself to the food in the kitchen?

She wondered if the situation were reversed - would she have been as hospitable as Kevin had been? How would she have reacted to a stranger asking to stay in her house?

Okay, after two days of talking and sharing their innermost secrets and most painful memories, Kevin and Sarah were hardly strangers. In two days she felt like she'd known him all her life.

Did he feel the same? *He had to*, she quickly decided. No one would let a complete stranger into their house unless he knew her. She took a deep breath and slipped off her shoes, then lay down on the bed. Briefly, she thought about texting Emily to let her know she was at Kevin's, but she thought better of it. She was far too embarrassed by her childish behavior. Kate acted like an ass, and Sarah ran away, punishing Emily in the process. What a mess. Then she closed her eyes.

The knock on the door woke her up. "Sarah?" Kevin said from outside door.

She sat up and pushed her hair back from her face. "Hold on a second," she said, hoping it was loud enough and feeling like she could slip back into a coma at any moment.

In the bathroom, she rinsed her face and smoothed her hair.

She looked awful and pale.

Finally, she went to the door and opened it a crack. "I'm sorry, did I wake you?" He stood patiently outside the door with a tray.

"Yeah, that's okay. I didn't want to sleep all day."

"You obviously needed it. It's already past seven. I thought you might want some dinner," he said.

That's when she realized the drapes in the room had been drawn and the bedside lamps were on.

"I had Beth check on you earlier to make sure you were all right."

"Oh, I'm sorry."

"Don't be ridiculous. There's nothing to be sorry for."

She opened the door completely and he carried the covered tray into the room, setting it on the desk in the far corner. Sarah followed.

Lifting the lid of the tray, he revealed a plate containing a pork chop, mashed potatoes, and green beans. Next to it was a proper maroon napkin with a fork and knife. "I'm not much of a chef, but I can cook a nice homemade meal like the best of them."

The smile she gave him came easily. "It looks wonderful."

"Oh, one last thing." He went back into the hallway and came

back almost immediately with a wine glass and a small carafe of wine. "Dinner wouldn't be dinner without wine."

She gave him and the meal a grateful smile. "Thank you, I feel like I'm imposing..."

"You look exhausted. Go ahead and eat and feel free to go back to bed when you're done. I can send Beth up for the tray in the morning. She's already gone home for the day." He put a reassuring hand on her shoulder. "You'll feel better once you've had more sleep and a proper shower in the morning. You'll be right as rain. You had an emotionally draining day."

She really had. The fact that Kevin recognized it made her feel cared for. He was too good to be true. No wonder Kate had been so suspicious.

Kevin bade her goodnight and left her alone to her dinner. There was comfort in silence and knowing that Kevin was giving her space. She finished her dinner and changed into sweats and a tank top. Now she didn't feel all that tired anymore. Leaving the tray on the desk for Beth to carry downstairs seemed rude, so she decided to take it down herself.

The hallway was more of a long corridor with shaded lamps on the walls. All of them were lit so she could find her way to the stairs. At the top of the staircase, she heard the television on in the living room.

In stocking feet, she padded down the stairs and to the kitchen, setting the tray gently on the counter.

"Sarah?" she heard his voice from the other room. "Yeah, it's just me. I thought I'd bring everything down tonight." The kitchen looked like a cyclone hit it. Three dirty pans sat on the stove and in the sink were the dishes. She opened the dishwasher, revealing that it was empty.

In that sense, Kevin was nothing like Eric. Eric always rinsed his dishes and put them in the dishwasher. Of course, Eric couldn't cook unless it involved a microwave or a barbecue.

Starting with the silverware, she rinsed them off and put them in the dishwasher, then moved to the plates.

"You don't have to do that," said Kevin from behind her. "Beth will take care of it in the morning."

"I should do something to earn my keep," she said, putting glasses in the top rack. "I would feel bad staying here only to freeload off of you."

He leaned on the counter and watched her, shaking his head. "Well, I won't argue. I'm sure Beth will be happy to know I haven't left her a huge mess to deal with. All the same, that's what I pay her for."

She didn't say anything, but continued to load the dishwasher. "So, dessert?"

"You made dessert?"

He chuckled. "You sound impressed."

"Most of the men I know are lucky if they can microwave macaroni and cheese," she told him matter-of-factly. "Don't take that to mean I think men can't do well in the kitchen, it's just none of the men I've known. Until now."

He went to the fridge and pulled out some cut strawberries and whipped cream, and produced a yellow sponge cake from a dark part of the counter. "I believe this to be strawberry shortcake. I also have chocolates if you prefer."

Sarah laughed. "Strawberry shortcake it is."

He grabbed two small plates from the cupboard and cut two slices of cake, then covered them with strawberries and whipped cream. "And here we are."

Then he got the forks.

She stopped cleaning up the kitchen, wiped her hands on a towel, and followed him to the table. "Dessert looks fantastic."

Together they sat at the breakfast nook table and ate dessert. Sarah looked him over. Even though he seemed happy on the outside, there was a deep sadness within him. It was something in his eyes. The pain of loss, she decided.

He caught her looking at him and shifted uncomfortably. "What is it?"

Pink hues crept into her cheeks. "What am I missing?"

His eyebrows lifted in response, giving way to a questioning look.

"I mean, you're a nice guy. You own your own business. You can cook…" She narrowed her eyes. "What's the deal breaker?"

He laughed. "Well, as you can see I'm a bit of a slob, which is why I employ a housekeeper."

She laughed. "Men like you are usually snapped right up by eligible women."

"Interesting. I could say the same about you."

"Oh yeah?"

He leaned in toward her. "You love horses, you're intelligent, you own your own business, and you're beautiful… what's the deal breaker?"

"I am too emotional and I can be very indecisive," she answered honestly.

"I can deal with that. So next let's look at what we both share. We're both business owners, we both like horses." He paused to see if she had anything to add.

"We both have had someone we love die." She didn't feel the urge to cry at all.

"We're both horribly damaged. I'm willing to bet we have even more in common. Would you like to watch television with me for a while before you head back to bed?"

That sounded fun. "What are you watching?"

"CSI," he said. "They show that here?"

"Streaming video," he said.

"Well, I love CSI," she told him with a smile as she took both of their now empty plates and used silverware to the sink for a rinse before she put them in the dishwasher. "So that's another thing we have in common."

"Do you read Stephen King novels?" His voice sounded hopeful.

With a laugh, she nodded. "I do, though admittedly I haven't read one in a few years."

A pleasant look of surprise washed over his face.

She finished straightening the kitchen, but only rinsed the pans, and when she was done, they made their way into the living room where the television was paused.

Kevin politely restarted the episode and they sat about a foot apart on the couch and watched television. When the next episode cued up, he made his move and put his arm over the back of the couch behind her and moved a little closer.

She felt like she was back in high school, nervous and awkward, and quite frankly - wanting to feel his touch, even if it was just an innocent kiss or embrace. Just like that, she scooted closer to him and put her head on his shoulder, then relaxed when she felt his arm come down around her. His body relaxed against hers and they stayed that way for another episode.

When it was over, she tried to stifle a yawn, but it didn't work. She didn't want the evening to end. No, she wasn't *that* tired despite the yawn, or, at least, that's what she tried to tell herself.

"You look exhausted. Maybe we should call it a night…" he started, a tinge of uncertainty in his voice.

Emily's words rang out in Sarah's mind. *Life is short, Sarah. Carpe diem. Seize the day,* she thought. Turning to Kevin, she wrapped her arms around his neck and pulled him to her, their lips pressing together in an innocent kiss that quickly turned more passionate. Kevin's lips found their way down her jawline to her neck, then back to her lips. Hungry for him, her hands explored his back and his strong biceps. Their tongues entwined in a lingering kiss that was only cut short because both of them needed to breathe.

Sarah's heart pounded in her chest. "I'm sorry," Kevin started. "I don't want to sleep alone tonight," Sarah told him, realizing

she'd just crossed the thresh-hold. There was no going back.

He didn't say anything at first.

A queasy feeling gripped her stomach.

Then she felt his embrace tighten around her and he pulled her to his chest and took a deep breath. "Okay, but all we do is sleep."

It felt so good to be this close to him. His masculine scent and strong arms comforted her. She felt safe like everything would be okay. "All right," she agreed.

They went upstairs and got ready for bed. She didn't need to change since the sweats and tank top are what she slept in anyway, and Kevin didn't protest or try to disrobe her. Instead, he pulled her close against him and held her. His soft breath was the only other sound in the room and for the first time in months she drifted to sleep in peace.

Eric stood in a bright light, his arms crossed over his chest. His eyes seemed to radiate that same white light.

"You couldn't wait, could you?"

"I thought you would want me to…" she started.

Kate, dressed in a flowing white gown, and floating three feet off the ground, interrupted her. "She's on the rebound. Willing to sleep with whoever."

"But we're not doing anything. Just sleeping."

"You let him kiss you like I kissed you," the image of Eric said. "He's not your replacement," Sarah protested.

"It's too soon. Everyone is going to judge you," dream Kate spat. "You're a whore."

"It's me or him, Sarah," Eric said.

For some reason, in the dream, it all seemed so desperate. Eric appeared alive - felt alive. Her heart pounded in her chest so hard she could hear it and she was crying, screaming.

"You're dead!" she cried. "Go away!"

"You never deserved Eric," dream Kate said in a disgusted tone. "I don't think I want to be your friend anymore."

Dream Kate's form started to vanish into thin air, and Sarah reached out to her. But then dream Eric caught her attention.

"Fine Sarah - I'll go." Eric started crying. "I loved you. Did you ever love me?"

"I did," she said, feeling a crying jag coming on.

She woke up with tears streaming down her face.

18

Into His Arms

The cottage felt like a tomb. Emily looked around and frowned. Now what was she going to do? She and Sarah had spent the morning having tea and watching television, waiting for Kate. It was the least they could do when they felt so bad for leaving her alone for dinner the night before. Then Kate just had to lose her temper like a mad woman and send Sarah packing. Literally.

Emily let out a deep sigh. Well, she couldn't stay here by herself. No, she didn't *want* to stay here by herself. It was too depressing. This wasn't how this trip was supposed to be. Before too long, Lucy and mom would start texting her, wondering why she wasn't sending pictures and she didn't want to have to explain Kate and Sarah's fight and have her mom worrying about her. Grabbing a jacket and her travel purse, she decided to go for a walk. She could get a few pictures to send and pretend that she was just enjoying a lazy day. It was colder today and she was glad she'd decided to wear jeans and a plain gray sweatshirt.

After locking up the cottage, she started up the hill toward Sean's. The first pangs of hunger hit her half way up. All she'd had the entire day were a few cookies, well - biscuits as the Irish called them, with her morning tea.

She didn't want to risk walking into town for fear of running into Kate again. She didn't want to fight with Kate, too. Right now she was the only bond between Kate and Sarah, the neutral observer. The market was on the outskirt of town, so if she could make it there, she could get some food and bring it back to the cottage and have a quiet dinner by herself. Everyone just needed their own space, she decided. Maybe that's why they'd all done their own thing yesterday.

Mrs. O'Flannigan must have seen her coming up the road because she stepped outside and grabbed her broom and began sweeping the porch again. This time, Emily caught it and smiled when she saw her, remembering Sean's explanation of his mother's excessive sweeping. Sean probably had to refinish the porch once a year at the rate his mother likely stripped it. She stifled a giggle.

"Hi Mrs. O'Flannigan," she said.

"Going for another walk today?" Mrs. O'Flannigan gave her a polite, inquisitive look.

"I was going to, but to be honest, I don't feel like walking all the way to the beach. I thought I'd go into town, get some food for dinner, and bring it back. Spend a quiet evening in." What she wanted was someone to talk to.

Mrs. O'Flannigan seemed to sense Emily's need to talk. "Would you like to come in for some tea?"

"I wouldn't want to impose…"

The older woman shook her head. "It's no trouble at all.

Come in."

She set the broom next to the door and motioned Emily inside. Gratefully, Emily went into the house, surprised at how modern and clean it was. For some reason, based on how Mrs. O'Flannigan dressed and how almost barren the outside of the house looked, she'd imagined the inside would be cluttered with family photographs and antique figurines or vases on every surface, or that the house would have old farmhouse furniture. Instead, there was a gray sectional sofa, modern end tables stained an oak color, and a big screen television.

The wood floors looked like they'd been recently redone, and the area rugs had modern looking designs in red and gold. She could see through to the dining room. The hutch and table both looked just as modern. The house smelled heavenly, as if Mrs. O'Flannigan had just cooked bacon.

"Sean has redone the entire house in the past five years.

Come, let me show you my new kitchen!" Mrs. O'Flannigan went ahead, leading Emily to the back of the house to the kitchen.

She wasn't kidding. The kitchen looked like a picture from a magazine with all stainless steel, state-of-the-art appliances and oak stained cupboards. Granite counter tops. Everything matched. "This is beautiful!"

"Sean has always been good at fixing things." She motioned Emily to sit.

So she did, and she watched as Mrs. O'Flannigan started the kettle. Not a traditional stove top tea kettle. It was a carafe she filled with water and plugged in. Evidently the heating element was inside it. Then she took out two tea cups and placed a tea bag in each. Emily tried to ignore the heavenly scent of whatever was in the oven but the lure was too strong. Her mouth watered and her hunger pangs became more urgent.

"Now," the older woman started. "Tell me about your friends. I heard they had an argument."

Emily studied the back of Sean's mom's head. She had blond hair and it was only now turning gray. She wasn't a day over sixty. Or didn't seem to be. She wondered if Sean was younger than she thought he was. When she realized Mrs. O'Flannigan was looking at her, waiting for an answer, she drew her attention back to their conversation. "You heard it?"

"Your friend, the short brunette. The sad one,

she walked

by here. Said she had an argument with Kate and was staying with a friend. Kevin, I believe his name was." Mrs. O'Flannigan didn't miss a single detail.

"Well, Kate was upset because last night Sarah had dinner with her friend Kevin, I had dinner with Sean, and Kate had to have dinner alone. And Kate also thinks Sarah isn't ready for a friend like Kevin right now. See, Sarah's fiancé passed away almost six months ago. Can I help with that?"

"No, dear. I've got it." She quickly turned the subject back onto Kate and Sarah. "I believe Kate told Sean that when she made the reservation for the cottage. That poor girl. What do you think about this Kevin?" The kettle light turned green and Mrs. O'Flannigan unplugged it and poured the hot water over each tea bag. "Would you like biscuits?"

"No, thank you, I'm done with biscuits for the day." She took the tea cup Mrs. O'Flannigan offered. "I haven't really talked to Kevin, but my understanding is they met horseback riding and, as it turns out, he lost his wife a few years ago. So he and Sarah have that loss in common."

"Ah. Kevin MacClery. Gabriella was such a sweet and beautiful young woman. To die that way was tragic and Mr. MacClery was devastated for months afterward. His housekeeper, Beth Murphy, was the only contact he had with the outside world, the poor man. But he got steadily better as the months passed. If anyone knows what Sarah is going through it would be him."

"Well, Kate thinks Kevin is taking advantage of Sarah's fragile state, and Sarah thinks Kate doesn't want her to be happy," Emily explained, pausing to take a sip of the tea.

She liked Irish tea. It wasn't as bitter as some of the teas back home. "It sounds ridiculous when I say it out loud like that."

"Well, I'm sure they'll be able to work it out. They just need to be apart for now."

Em nodded. "That's what I was thinking."

"It's unfortunate you've been caught in the middle," the older woman went on.

A soft chime emanated from Emily's pocket. She pulled out her phone. "Sorry, I don't mean to be rude, but it might be my daughter. Do you mind if I check?"

"Not at all. I think it's wonderful you can be a continent apart and still be able to connect with your family by a cellular phone. Sean keeps trying to get me to get one." She shrugged, trying to look over and see what was on the phone screen.

It was Lucy, and sure enough, she was asking why she hadn't gotten any pictures today. "Lucy wants to know why I haven't sent her pictures today, but I can't very well tell her Sarah and Kate are fighting."

"How old is she?" It was the quintessential question everyone asked when they found out one had kids.

"Twelve."

"And how old are you?" That was not usually the question someone asked.

"Thirty-four."

"You married young."

"I suppose I did. I was only twenty-two and fresh out of college. Worst mistake of my life." Then she realized who she was talking to. "I mean my marriage. Not my daughter. My daughter was the only good thing that came of my marriage."

"How long have you been divorced?" The questions were starting to sound carefully planned now. She remembered how Sean told her how clever his mother was. Undoubtedly Sean's mom wanted to know more about the woman who had spent an afternoon and evening with her son. It was only one day.

"About a year now. But the marriage was over almost three years ago." She gave Sean's mom a weak smile. A lot of Irish were fiercely Catholic, and divorce was still frowned upon by those who were devout.

Luckily Sean's mom, while she appeared to be Catholic as evidenced by the crucifix hanging around her neck, didn't seem to be one of the zealous ones. "Well that's unfortunate, but you're still young. You might still remarry and have more children."

"Maybe. It would be nice to have another baby or two. I know Lucy would love to have siblings though she'd be grown and out of the house by the time they were old enough for her to be interested in them as people." She smiled at the thought. "My mom would love to have more grandchildren for sure."

Mrs. O'Flannigan smiled as if remembering. "I wish I had grandchildren. I'd be happy to have at least one."

"How many kids do you have?"

"Only Sean. He's good to come home and help me here, but I worry he'll never marry. He's thirty-six already and he's not even proposed to a woman." She sighed heavily.

This was dangerous territory. Emily decided to tread lightly. "Well, thirty-six is still young. A lot of couples are waiting to have kids until their mid to late thirties.

Sometimes even their forties." She wasn't sure what else to say.

Mrs. O'Flannigan sipped her tea, then shook her head. "No, I'm afraid no woman will want to take on a husband who has a sheep farm and his mother to look after."

"That's not true. I think any woman who loves a man would accept his family and his vocation no matter what it was. I know I would. Besides, what if she likes sheep?" Emily gave her a satisfied smile.

Mrs. O'Flannigan returned the smile. "Perhaps you should date my son."

"Well, he already took me sightseeing and to dinner, though I don't think that qualifies as a date," she lied. The kiss in the truck afterward told a different story, but she certainly wasn't telling his mother that. "Doesn't he, at least, date women regularly?"

"He dated a girl for a time, it seems like it was more than a year ago, but she wanted to live in Dublin and she wanted him to sell and convince me to move to a flat in Galway near my sister. I thought of doing it just so he could have a life, but he said he didn't want to. He wanted to stay here. He's a good son." Mrs. O'Flannigan looked somewhat weary then. "He is, isn't he?" Emily agreed.

"All the more reason you should go out with him again."

"Mrs. O'Flannigan," Emily started.

"Call me Ellis, dear. Mrs. O'Flannigan is so formal."

"Ellis, I have to admit that I like Sean. I do. I'd love to go out with him, but I live across the ocean. I'm afraid that even if Sean and I *dated* while I was here, I'd be nothing more than a fling." She frowned at the thought. Her hopes of anything with Sean, even sex, crumbled. How could she have deluded herself? She could never have him, not knowing what she knew. He deserved more than a vacationing divorcee who hadn't had sex in at least two years. "But we can always be friends."

"Of course, my dear." Ellis reached across the table and patted the back of Emily's hand. That's when Sean walked through the front door.

"That fence is fine," he said, not realizing Emily was sitting there. "I think Thomas left the gate open."

When he saw Emily he did a double take and a slow smile spread over his lips. "Emily. I wasn't expecting you."

"Her friends are having a bit of an argument." Ellis got up and followed him to the kitchen. "Would you like some tea before dinner?"

Sean pretended like Emily being in the house was no big thing, but she could tell he was a bit nervous by the way he avoided eye contact. He went to the sink and washed his hands. "Nah, I thought maybe I'd clean up and grab a pint with the lads. Aedan's off tonight."

"Just as well. I thought I'd invite Emily to have dinner with me. I'm enjoying her company. Are you sure you won't, at least, stay for dinner?" Ellis was crafty.

He looked at his mother, then at Emily, then dried his hands. "What'd you make?"

"Hot pot." Ellis looked at her. "Would you stay and have dinner with me?"

Emily didn't want to be rude, and she was starving. It would certainly save her from having to walk to the store and back. "As long as it's no trouble."

"It's no trouble at all. And you?" She turned to Sean. "I guess I can stay for dinner."

"You'll have some tea now, too?" Ellis went for the tea. "I can make my own tea," Sean assured her. "You don't have to wait on me hand and foot. I know how to make tea."

"Oh dear, don't forget to let your daughter know that you're all right," Ellis reminded her.

Emily had completely forgotten the phone. She took it out of her pocket and sent Lucy a quick text letting her know that she was having dinner with a friend.

"The same guy from last night? He's cute, Mom," said the reply.

She texted back a single word. "Yes."

Then she put her phone back in her pocket and fought back that resigned sigh she felt building in her chest.

Resigned because even though she wanted Sean, she knew they could only be friends. Unless he was just looking for friends with benefits. If that were the case, then it might work. Her thoughts were cut off by a ringing phone. It was Sean's cell. He excused himself and left the room.

Ellis came back to the table to see if their tea needed refilling. When she saw Emily's cup was almost empty, she immediately snatched it up and went to make her a new cup.

Sean returned and went to retrieve his tea. "Who was it then?" his mother asked.

"Aedan." He turned to Emily. "It seems he ran into Kate at the pub. He thought she needed a friend, so he was canceling with me."

"It's just as well," Ellis said with a knowing smile. "Now we can have a nice dinner."

Emily couldn't just sit there. "Can I help set the table or anything?"

Ellis brought her a new cup of tea. "Stay here. I'll take care of it. You and Sean just sit here and have a nice conversation."

Sean looked across the table at Emily and she looked at him and shrugged.

He laughed under his breath.

Taking the casserole out of the oven, Sean's mom set it on the stove to cool. "Now, give it five minutes and I'll serve it, but I think I need to use the loo."

Just like that, Ellis excused herself from the room to another part of the house.

"I told you she was…"

"Crafty?" Emily finished.

Sean thought about her word choice for a second and nodded. "Has she asked you to date me yet?"

Emily winced.

"Oh God she has." He shook his head. "I'm sorry." She laughed. "No, it's okay."

"How about I put dinner on plates." He got up, clearly uncomfortable.

"Let me help." She followed him to the counter. "Can I get the forks and knives?"

"You won't need a knife for Mum's hot pot. She cuts everything into bite sizes," he assured her, and then he pointed out the drawer where she could find forks.

Taking three forks from the drawer, now they needed napkins. "Paper napkins?"

He pointed to another cupboard. With napkins and forks in place, she helped him bring the filled plates to the table. They finished just as Ellis returned.

"You both are so helpful. Thank you." She took her place at the table between them. "Now, let's say grace."

Sean bowed his head and Emily did the same. While she was born into a Catholic family and baptized the same, her family had never been observant at any time other than Christmas or Easter. Something she'd never put much thought into until now.

"For the bounty laid before us, may the Lord make us thankful, and ever mindful of the needs of others. Amen." Ellis lifted her head. "Are you Catholic, dear?"

"Yes, but not observing." She felt like she should explain herself. "My family only goes to church on Easter and Christmas. But I was baptized so I suppose at some point they were observant."

"You never had your daughter baptized then?"

"Mum, you can't ask those kinds of questions," Sean started, clearly embarrassed.

"No, it's all right. Lucy was never baptized. Her father never went to church and always said he didn't believe in organized religion," she told her. Her lack of religion wasn't an embarrassment to her.

"So Martin will be by to check on the lambs next week, but I think they're doing well." Sean expertly changed the subject, taking Ellis' questioning away from Emily, for which Emily was thankful.

Sean seemed to be grateful for the change in topic, too.

They talked about sheep for three-quarters of the meal, then there was a lull in the conversation.

Finally, Emily said, "What else would you recommend we
see while we're here?"

"You're expecting your friends will reconcile?" Ellis asked. "Absolutely. They both just need time to cool off," Emily
said, hoping she was right.

"Would you like more?" Ellis asked, pointing to Emily's empty plate.

"Oh no. I couldn't. I'm stuffed, but it was wonderful. Thank you so much."

Ellis beamed at her. "Thank you, dear."

"I'll clean the kitchen," Emily offered. Sean jumped in, "I'll help."

"Oh? Well, I suppose I'll leave you both to it then." Just like that Ellis got up and left the room. She wasn't subtle by any means.

Emily giggled and shook her head. "Your mother is... very sweet."

"Yes, well, it's too bad she likes to meddle."

"She only does it because she worries about you.

Thinks you've given up your life to take care of her." Emily got up and piled the empty plates on top of one another with the silverware on top, and took them to the sink.

Sean followed with the glasses and used paper napkins.

He tossed the napkins into the trash bin then took the glasses to the sink.

"So after we finish the dishes would you like to come over and watch a movie? Netflix?" He sounded somewhat unsure of himself. Perhaps it was fear of possible rejection.

Her heart quickened. "Are you asking me to your apartment?"

Of course she knew Ellis wouldn't care. If anything, she might have insisted.

"Yes."

"Okay. But you do realize that I'm leaving in a couple of weeks and whatever happens is just…" Even though she knew he was a grown man capable of making his own decisions, she didn't want to lead him on and make him think it was more than it was.

"What do you think is going to happen?" Sean asked with a chuckle.

Emily blushed. "I never said anything would happen, only that if it did, then it would be… temporary."

"One of those vacation romances I keep hearing about." She couldn't help but laugh.

"I'll chance it," he said. "Of course, never say never."

"What
do you mean?" She had almost all the dishes rinsed and in the dishwasher.

"That something more can come from this."

"I don't want to lead you on because you deserve more." She gave him a half-hearted smile. "I'm leaving in a couple of weeks."

"I know, but there's only an ocean."

"That's a big deal to a lot of people. Expensive." There was certainly no way she could afford to keep traveling back and forth.

"I think we should play it by ear, see what happens. No harm in that." He looked at the clock. "In the meantime, we have time for some movies."

"What's your favorite genre?" She wiped down the counters. He put the leftovers away.

Then he handed her the empty baking dish. "Science fiction."

"Lucy likes that too. I've been formally educated in *Star Wars* versus *Star Trek*." Taking the pan from him, she put it in the sink and ran some water over it, then used the scrub brush to loosen the food particles. This could go in the dishwasher, too, but it would have to be properly washed first.

Sean laughed. "Good. That will make it easier."

She laughed right along with him. Once the kitchen was cleaned, with a hollered goodbye to Ellis, he led Emily out the back kitchen door, down some steps and into his bachelor apartment. When he flicked on the light, several lamps in the room came on, lighting up the apartment significantly.

Sean wasn't a slob. In fact, he seemed rather neat and tidy. He even had a special tray for his keys near the door. An automated air freshener sat on top of a bookshelf near the window and sprayed an apple cinnamon scent into the room.

"Your mom's idea?"

He nodded. "Yes, how did you know?"

"It's a female thing," she said.

Everything looked tidy and felt comfortable. It wasn't sticky or dirty or damp or smelly like she remembered some guy's apartments back in college.

She went over to the bookshelf and started reading off titles. Sean was well-read or appeared to be. He had everything from bestsellers to science fiction novels, to non-fiction how-to books. A few science magazines sat on the coffee table. He was clearly still interested in science.

Emily took a seat on the sofa without asking. "Would you like a beer?"

"Sure," she said, picking up the magazine. The headline read *The Vaccination Debate*. He returned from the small galley kitchenette off the living room with two cans of Guinness.

The apartment only had a bathroom, a bedroom, the living room, and the kitchenette. But honestly - what more did he need?

He sat down and set the beers on the coffee table, then noticed she'd been looking at the magazine.

"You still keep up with scientific studies."

With a nod, he opened his beer and grabbed the remote. "Yeah."

It was strange because sometimes he sounded Irish, like *really* Irish, and other times when he spoke he almost had a perfect American accent. Em found it disarming. She would momentarily forget she was in a foreign country and the man next to her lived an ocean, and half a continent, away.

"Any chance you'd ever go back into science?" She was genuinely curious.

"Likely not at this point in my life since I've been out of it so long, but the interest is still there. What about you? Are you doing what you thought you'd be doing when you were in college?"

She shrugged. "Yes and no. I am working in the area I thought I would be, but I don't care for it as much as I thought I would. I'll probably have a midlife crisis, throw caution to the wind, and buy a sports car. Perhaps do something crazy - like visit a nudist colony."

He laughed and clicked on the television. "Hopefully not anytime soon."

"No, I have about ten to fifteen years to go before that happens." Talking to Sean felt easy and natural. Like they'd been friends for far longer than they actually had been.

That's what it was like when two people clicked, she remembered. It had been so long since she'd had this kind of conversation with a man.

Even looking back, she realized she and Sam had similar conversations, but she always felt awkward during them. Like she wasn't saying the right thing. It wasn't like that with Sean. With him, she felt she could be honest and open and he wouldn't judge her.

"We have time to defuse the ticking bomb then." She laughed. "We can hope."

Turning her attention to the television, she watched him navigate a familiar *Netflix* screen to some new releases. One of them a remake of a popular sci-fi flick from the eighties. Lucy had seen it and loved it. By the way he hovered there, she could tell he was debating whether or not to ask her if she wanted to watch it.

"Lucy really liked that one," she told him. "If you haven't seen it, we should watch it. I haven't seen it either."

"Are you sure?"

"Of course."

She wasn't sure why she did it, but she moved over on the couch closer to him, probably so she could reach her beer. She opened it and took a sip and set it back on the table. When she leaned back, she noticed his arm draped in comfort over the back of the couch. Upon making herself comfortable, their knees touched and she made no move to pull her knee away, thankful he didn't either.

In her head, she chastised herself for acting like a giddy schoolgirl. But the reality was there, staring her in the face.

She liked Sean O'Flannigan and even though her rational brain told her that a romance with him was a bad, bad idea, her body told a different story, and it was winning the argument.

In her head, different scenarios played their way out, causing focus on the movie impossible. She didn't care about half-human cyborgs in a future dictatorship world. For the first time since before Lucy was born, she felt alive, sexy, vibrant. Her own imagination fueled her desire making it harder and harder to just sit there with him.

This was the reason she put her hand on his knee and made the first move. "You're going to have to watch this later."

Sean paused the movie and looked at her, getting ready to ask something.

Emily planted a kiss on his lips and relaxed into him when she felt his arms encircle her and his hand move down her back to her backside.

That's how Emily ended up spending the night with Sean O'Flannigan.

19

The Fall

Sarah sat straight up in bed, tears stinging her eyes. She found the glowing green numbers on the alarm clock and realized it was six thirty in the morning.

Kevin mumbled something and rolled over. She was thankful she hadn't woken him.

Slipping from the room, she made her way to her own room to put on a change of clothes. Kevin wouldn't mind if she went riding by herself, would he? She didn't want to wake him but she needed to clear her mind and a morning ride was the perfect thing. Before she left, she decided to leave a note on the kitchen table. It said: *Have gone riding down to the beach. Will be back for breakfast.*

None of the stable hands were at the barn when she arrived, so she let herself into the tack room, and with an armful of saddle and bridle, found Pickle's stall quite easily.

"Hey Pickles!" she greeted the mare.

Pickles snorted and nuzzled her with her velvety muzzle. The mare already wore a blue halter, making her easy to catch and bring out for saddling. It helped that Pickles was a gentle horse and more than willing to go.

Just a ride down by the sea. It would calm her nerves after the dream. Of course, she knew Eric would have never denied her happiness. The dream was simply a reflection of her fears. It wasn't like she had intercourse with Kevin though she knew that was coming. How couldn't it after they'd bared their souls to one another, kissed and slept in the same bed? She felt the familiar stirrings in her loins whenever their bodies touched. She was attracted to him, and not only because of their shared grief. No, Kevin was a very handsome man and they had enough in common that it could work. Even without Eric and Gabriella, he was her type, and it appeared she was his.

The mare, now properly saddled, seemed to welcome such an early morning ride. Sarah made sure the horse wasn't holding air and re-checked the girth, then mounted. With the gentle nudge of her heels, Pickles started forward, away from the house and toward the trail down to the beach. The clouds seemed to ebb and flow. She wondered if the gray morning would give way to a sunny afternoon or if they'd get rain.

Winds picked up as she crested the hill where the trail began descending downward. Carefully, Pickles picked her way, sure-footed, along the trail toward the beach with Sarah on her back enjoying the wind against her face. She relaxed into Pickles' movements and felt at one with the horse. She could get used to this. A boyfriend with horses who lived near the ocean in another country. More and more, it felt like she could do this - could make this relationship work. After all, she had a flexible job and money. So did he. They could easily make living together doable. They could have a house in the States and the house here.

Doubt crept in again, annoying as it was. *You're a dreamer,* her mind screamed. *Yes, but a pragmatic one,* she told herself. Ever since she was young, she had always had her head in the clouds, but her feet firmly planted on the ground. All of her friends and family had said that it was because of that Sarah had been so successful in everything she did.

Closing her eyes, she let the horse continue along the trail. She removed her right foot from the stirrups to stretch out her ankle and relax. That's when the plastic bag came out of nowhere, whipping onto the trail like a snake, causing Pickles to jump and bolt, throwing Sarah straight into the pile of rocks on the side of the trail. She wasn't wearing a helmet.

***

Emily grabbed a notepad from her bag and a pen and started writing down what Kevin was telling her.

"Do you have someone who can bring you here?" Kevin asked.

"Kate's here. We have the car," she assured him.

"I'd rather you had someone drive you both," he said. He sounded worried and tired, with fear on the edge of his voice.

"If we can't manage I have a friend who might be able to help." As soon as she said it she felt that familiar pang of guilt. How could she ask Sean? But if Kate couldn't drive, Sean would have to because there was no way Emily was going to remain calm enough to be able to find the hospital. "We'll be there soon."

She hung up and turned to Kate. "It's Sarah, there was an accident."

With a deep breath and a sob, she began crying, unable to stop herself.

"What happened?" The look on Kate's face was panicked. "Sarah went for a ride this morning. She was thrown from

the horse and she wasn't wearing a helmet. Right now they can't wake her up." Her voice trailed off into nothing and she sucked in a ragged breath, vaguely aware of the tears welling in Kate's eyes.

"We have to go, what's the address?" Kate sprang into action and pulled out her phone.

She handed the piece of paper with the address to Kate. "We have to say we're her sisters so they'll let us see her.

Kevin had to tell them he was her husband, or they wouldn't let him in. It's family only."

Kate typed the address into the phone, waiting for the GPS to kick in. "God damn thing!"

Her frustration turned to tears until she threw the phone on the ground, luckily not breaking it.

"Okay," Emily said, trying to calm herself and Kate. "We're just going to go up to Sean's and see if he can drive us."

Kate picked up the phone and nodded. "Okay."

Together, they left the cottage and went up the road to the O'Flannigan place. He was outside with one of the dogs, unloading a few bags of dog food from the back of the truck.

Sean smiled when he saw her. "You were up bright and early."

"Kate got home early," she lied. "But we need your help and I know it's not fair to ask, but Sarah is in the hospital and we need to get there, but our GPS isn't working so we don't know how to get there."

His eyes went from Emily to Kate and back again. Undoubtedly he saw how frazzled they both were. They must have looked awful with their red eyes and tears. "Is she okay?"

"We don't know."

"Get in the truck." He ran into the house and came back out, followed by Ellis, who waved from the door.

When he joined them in the truck, he had his phone. "Which hospital is it?"

"Galway Hospital. She's in the trauma center."

They started off. In a small voice, Kate asked, "Is that like an ICU?"

Emily nodded. It was all she could do. She'd taken the seat next to Sean. When he reached out and took her hand into his and squeezed, she didn't pull away.

"What happened?" he asked.

"She went riding this morning by herself, not wearing a helmet, and something happened and she fell off. She hit her head." She found herself staring at the passing landscape, numb to it. "Kevin woke up and saw she'd gone out. She left a note letting him know she went riding down to the beach. Then the horse showed back up at his place without her and he knew something was wrong, so he went out after her and found her."

"Thank goodness she left a note with where she'd gone so he could find her," Sean said.

Again, Emily just nodded. She wasn't sure whether or not that was a jab at her disappearing trick early that morning, but she didn't care. There were more important things to worry about right now.

The ride through mid-morning traffic seemed to take forever, but they finally reached the hospital. Sean went in with them, to the main desk. The doe-eyed girl behind the reception desk ignored them at first.

"Excuse me, our sister was just brought here and we need to know where we can find her," Emily said matter-of-factly.

"What is her name please?"

"Sarah May."

"She's in the traumatic injury ward, but it seems they have put in a transfer to neurology," the woman said her voice void of passion or interest.

"Emily? Kate?" came a rather dignified male voice from behind them.

They turned around to see Kevin.

"I thought that was you. Come with me. I just came down for some coffee. They had me sitting in a waiting room. Perhaps you should get something to drink before you go up," he suggested, clearly expecting it to be awhile before the doctors got to them.

"Have they done x-rays?" Kate asked.

Kevin nodded. "They have done x-rays. I wanted to move her to a private hospital so we could get better communication, but I was assured some of the best neurologists are here. If that proves not to be the case, we'll have her moved as long as she's stable."

He seemed to have it all worked out, for which Emily was thankful. She wasn't sure what she'd do if she were asked to make these types of decisions right now.

Kevin looked beyond the women. "Hello."

Surprised, Emily turned around to see Sean still standing there. Then she remembered her manners. "Sean, this is Kevin. Kevin, Sean."

The men greeted one another.

"As far as the hospital is concerned, you're now Sarah's brother or brother-in-law. It was the only way they'd tell me anything is if I said I was her husband. Family only, which is why I suggested you claim to be her sisters. It's not as if they'll make you try to prove it."

"Well, we are like sisters," Kate said. "We even fight like sisters."

It was clear that Kate was still feeling horrible about the things she'd said that caused her and Sarah to fight, and Emily hoped more than anything that they'd have a chance to reconcile. God forbid anything bad happen.

Neither she nor Kate wanted a beverage, so they followed Kevin, with Sean in tow, to the elevator and to the ward where Sarah was. They weren't allowed to go in.

Instead, Kevin stopped at a reception station and said, "These are Sarah's sisters, and her brother-in-law. Any word on when we can see her yet?"

The red-head gave them a pleasant smile. "If you'll wait in the waiting room I'm sure the doctor will be out in a bit."

"Thank you," Kevin said, turning and heading straight into the waiting room.

Waiting rooms were never as comfortable as they tried to make them. The vinyl chairs and faux plants, combined with large windows to let in the gray of the day, and the awful earth-tones made the whole situation worse. There was nothing cheerful or comforting in the room. None of them spoke, but Emily could see Kevin was worried. He began pacing the length of the waiting room, making Sean a bit nervous.

Sean took the chair next to Emily and took her hand into his. "I'll stay until you know what's going on, then I can arrange to pick you both up and bring you back as needed."

"I feel horrible having you do that," Emily started. "I want to do it."

Kate stared off into the grayness beyond the windows with eyes that saw nothing.

The doctor acknowledged Kevin first. "Mr. MacClery."

"Yes." Kevin paused and pointed to Kate and Emily.

"These are her sisters and her brother-in-law."

The doctor, a short graying man with a mustache, addressed all of them. "We initially thought maybe she had a brain bleed, but we're not seeing that in the x-rays.

Instead, it appears to be a concussion, but we're concerned because we can't seem to wake her up. However, the injury doesn't appear severe enough to have caused a coma, so right now we just need to wait and see what happens. Brain injuries are tricky. She does have a fractured wrist and some bruises. So when she wakes up, she'll likely be sore, but we just need her to wake up so we can see what we're dealing with and to what severity."

"When can we see her?"

"We are going to move her into our neurology ward, and it will take us a while to get her settled." He stopped and glanced at his watch. "Go to wing B, second floor, room three-ten at around two o'clock and she should be there. Visiting hours are until eight."

Kevin had produced a notebook and wrote it all down. "Now I suggest maybe you all go to the cafeteria and have some lunch if you're able to. There's nothing you can do. I know waiting is the hardest part. It is for all of us." The doctor nodded at them and then turned and left.

Then Kevin, whose manner of dress and speech pegged him as someone who had likely never worked a blue collar job his entire life, herded them from the room and back toward the elevators.

"But I'm not hungry," Kate protested.

"You should, at least, have some tea or coffee and maybe a roll," said Kevin. "If you don't, the hunger will hit you when you least expect it. You have to keep your strength. They'll call me if anything changes. They have my number."

"You've done this before," Sean commented.

"I spent the last year of my wife's life in the hospital with her. You learn very quickly how to advocate for your loved one. If you don't, no one else will." Kevin led them to the cafeteria and found them a clean table in a corner. "Now, what can I get all of you?"

"Coffee," Kate said.

"Tea, with milk," Emily said.

Sean started off with Kevin. "I'll go with you to bring it back."

The silence between her and Kate felt deafening. "Are we seriously just going to sit here?" Kate finally asked.

"There's nothing else we can do," Emily said, letting out a deep sigh. She looked to Kevin and Sean and noticed they were having a conversation that, from their facial expressions, seemed pleasant.

"What do you think they're saying? Do you think he's withholding information?" Kate's nervous question-asking was enough to drive a person crazy, but Emily didn't mind.

There was something comforting in Kate's voice. At least they were there together. She pulled her phone from her pocket and decided to text her mom. "Lucy and mom will be wondering why I haven't sent pictures today.

Yesterday I took a picture of the field behind Sean's and said I was having dinner and a movie with a friend and they seemed okay with that."

She knew that Lucy would start hounding her mom for more pictures before too long.

"You could always take a picture of Kevin and Sean waiting for beverages and me sitting at this tiny table in this chair. Is it me or are these the most uncomfortable chairs you've ever sat in? What if we're down here screwing off and something bad is happening to Sarah right now?" Kate's voice verged on the edge of panic and she started wringing her hands.

Emily wasn't sure Kate realized she was doing it.

Reaching into her purse, she pulled out a tube of lotion and handed it to Kate. "Your hands look dry. Try this."

"Seriously, Em! She could be dying."

With a quick head shake, Emily looked her friend straight in the eyes. "Kate, it's going to be okay. It's probably just a bad concussion. You heard the doctor. It's not a brain bleed and that's good. We just need her to wake up. If anything happens they have Kevin's cellular number and they can call us. We can get right back up there. The truth of the matter is whether we're here or there, whatever happens, is going to happen. It's in God's hands now."

Kate's jaw dropped then she cringed. "I never thought I'd hear you get all religious on me."

It was no secret Kate was borderline atheist. She'd never been adamant about it or pushy with it, but her reaction to Emily's comment made Emily want to laugh. It brought a broad smile to her lips. "Well, I was baptized Catholic. Sean is Catholic."

Kate laughed, nervously at first, but then she fell into an uncontrollable fit.

"What's so funny about that? It wasn't funny."

When Kate finally regained her composure, she sighed. "You crack me up. Of the three of us, you were the last one I'd have thought would hook up with a guy."

"Sarah did, too," Emily said, nodding toward Kevin. "I don't think she slept with him." Kate shook her head.

With a wrinkled nose, Emily frowned. "How do you know? She slept at his place last night."

"Yeah, and I slept at Aedan's, on the couch. I woke up with a hangover on his couch, too. Truth be told, I honestly thought I would have been the one to meet a guy and hook up." Kate shrugged as if she'd put a lot of thought into this. "Let's face it Em, of the three of us, I'm the one with the bad habit of picking up one night stands."

"Sean wasn't a one-night stand."

"Wasn't he?" Kate smiled, then it vanished as if she just remembered where they were. Now was not a time for merriment.

"I'd do it again. That was the best sex I've had since

college."

"You didn't have sex in college."

Emily couldn't stifle the inappropriate laugh. "I did too." Kate shook her head. "Besides Sam, who?"

"That one guy…" her voice trailed off as the men came back to the table, both carrying drinks.

"*That one guy* my arse," Kate said under her breath, but Emily heard.

Too bad Sarah wasn't awake and here with them. This was the type of conversation that would have sent her into hysterical laughter and plenty of girl banter would ensue.

"So how pissed was Sarah at me?" Kate asked Kevin. "I hope I wasn't responsible."

Kate looked down at her cup, suddenly sober and devoid of all happiness. That's sometimes how it was with her. Especially when it came to emotional things. Kate was flighty like that.

He shook his head. "She just needed some time away to collect her thoughts. I never expected she'd stay more than a night or two before going back to stay at your cottage. I don't think what happened was anyone's fault. Sarah is a competent rider and the horse she was riding is very gentle and easy going. But it was windy and my guess is something spooked the horse and Sarah wasn't expecting it. It was an accident. She's going through a lot right now."

Kevin's eyes traveled to the window on the other side of the room and he looked out. "She probably just wanted some alone time."

"Thank goodness she left the note," Sean said.

With a nod, Kevin agreed. "Yes, it gave me an idea of the trail she took. I'm glad the mare came back like she did. She was probably wanting her morning breakfast."

His phone rang. He looked at the screen and lifted an eyebrow. "It's the hospital."

He answered in that smooth, refined accent that Emily imagined could only be learned in some affluent prep-school. They all listened for any indication of what was being said on the other end.

"We'll be up there straight away. Thank you," he said before hanging up and slipping the phone in his pocket in one smooth motion. Looking into their waiting faces, he paused, perhaps for dramatic effect, or perhaps because he wanted to make sure he said it right. "She's awake and they now have her in Room three-ten, second floor, ward B. Evidently she woke up when they transferred her to the bed. Must have jostled her from sleep."

In a cacophony of chairs scraping linoleum, they all got up and started toward the elevators. Emily's first thought was that she was thankful Sarah was alive and awake. Her second thought was that she was glad Sarah had good insurance.

When they reached the room, they found Sarah propped up on pillows fading in and out of sleep. The doctor was there checking up on her. When they entered, he nodded and patted Sarah on the shoulder. Her right hand was in a cast, probably for the fractured wrist. That sucked for Sarah, no more riding this vacation, Emily thought.

Sarah seemed to be fighting to stay awake. "She's responding in the way I want her to be, suggesting no permanent injury and nothing more serious than a bad concussion. She'll likely be drifting in and out. We obviously need to keep her overnight for observation and I want her to get some rest, but you can all say hello and then come back tomorrow," the doctor told them.

Emily wasn't comfortable with that at all. "Shouldn't one of us stay?"

"I'll stay," Kevin said, his tone insistent. By the look on his face she could tell he was worried about her. Emily wondered then if he was worried about losing another woman he loved, because that's how he acted.

"Very well. I think allowing her husband to stay near her until visiting hours are over won't do any harm, but I don't want her distracted from rest," the physician said before excusing himself from the room.

"Maybe we should..." Kate started.

Kevin cut her off. "No, really, I insist. You both look tired. It's been a stressful day. I can stay and when she's released, I can bring her back to the cottage if that's where she wants to go."

"But someone is going to have to help her with her insurance paperwork and how it all works with regard to her health insurance. We also have traveling insurance," Emily said, not sounding the least bit convincing. She was tired and while she wanted to stay with Sarah, sitting there holding vigil by Sarah's bedside likely wasn't going to accomplish anything while Sarah was sleeping and recovering from the fall.

"That's all taken care of," Kevin said. His tone had a finality to it. The matter was settled.

Sean sat quietly by as a beacon of support, and Emily wondered how off schedule he was, dealing with the sheep today. She knew animal husbandry wasn't something you could put off. Of course, it had appeared they caught him just as he was finishing his morning chores. It was only quarter after two now. He still had plenty of time to take care of the sheep when he got home, she assured herself. He excused himself to the hallway.

Then her attention turned to Sarah, and she moved to Sarah's bedside with Kate close at her heels. Sarah's eyes fluttered open. "Hey, girl. You took a nasty fall off that horse, but the doctor thinks you're going to be okay."

Sarah tried to nod, but winced when she did, a sure sign her head hurt.

"No, don't nod," Kate said, wincing with her. "I know this isn't the time or place, but I'm so sorry I said those things I said. It was incredibly selfish for me to be upset and I didn't mean any of it."

Tears brimmed Kate's eyes. "I'm just so happy you're going to be okay."

Sarah's eyes opened wider and she gave Emily a look that said, *what is she going on about?* It was clear to Emily that Sarah was already over her and Kate's argument. That's how Sarah was. Just like Emily suspected, they just needed space and time away from one another.

Sean returned a few minutes later.

After careful hugs and parting words of encouragement, a nod from Sean and a well-wish, the nurse came in and kicked all but Kevin out of the room.

The ride back to the cottage was quiet. Emily could feel her yearning for Sean's embrace, for comfort's sake. She wanted to lean against him and feel his strong arms around her, feel his fingers stroke her hair.

They found the cottage with the door open and Mrs. O'Flannigan coming out the front door. Together, they all filed from the truck. Kate seemed anxious at the intrusion of their privacy, but she didn't say anything. Emily could see it in her face and by how she fidgeted.

"Aedan sent over dinner and I told him I'd put it inside for you. You both go on in and eat and get some rest." The elder woman reminded Emily of her own mother now. The way she looked over them as if they were lost sheep needing guidance.

"I'll check on you after I've finished my chores for the night," Sean said.

"Thanks, Sean," Emily said, wanting to hug him, but not in front of his mother. It just didn't feel right.

He smiled, helped his mother into the truck, and they were back up the hill to their house that quickly.

"Holy crap," came Kate's voice from inside the cottage. Emily joined her, closing the door behind her. "What?" She saw the table set with a roast chicken, green beans, and roasted potatoes along with a bottle of wine, special tea, and two bowls of chocolate mousse.

It was the chocolate mousse that held the most interest for Em. "Your boyfriend really knows that a way to a woman's heart is through the chocolate."

Kate rolled her eyes then went back to reading whatever was on the paper she held in her hand. "He's just a friend."

"I think that's pretty cool. Imagine that — Kate has a male friend who's just a friend." She never imagined she'd see the day where that was the case.

The petite blonde seemed embarrassed. "Point taken, Em. Now let's eat before it gets cold."

"What's in the note?"

Kate debated whether or not she wanted to tell Emily, but

finally, she relented. "Aedan was just reiterating some sage advice he gave me, and wishing us well. Irish men are so polite."

Together, Emily and Kate sat down to dinner together, and they laughed and reminisced about college. The only thing missing were Sarah's tales of parties gone awry and her light laughter.

20

Reconciliation

Sarah woke up to find Kevin sitting next to her bed.

Her head still hurt a little and she felt disoriented as if she'd just emerged from a thick fog.

"What happened?"

Kevin reached out and took her hand into his. "You hit your head. This is the most lucid I've seen you since they moved you to this room."

"Well, I feel like I hit my head." She winced and looked around, recognizing the hospital room for what it was.

Bland, lifeless and mostly white or cream colored. Then she remembered. Pickles reared and bolted when Sarah's feet were out of the stirrups and she was thrown. "It was a bag in the wind."

He gave her a questioning look.

"Pickles. The wind blew a plastic bag onto the path and it scared her. She bolted just as I was adjusting my stirrups," she explained further, suddenly feeling a sharp pain in her right wrist. Looking down, she saw the cast. "I broke my wrist?"

"It's fractured." Kevin gave her a weak smile. "I'm glad to know it was an accident like I suspected."

"Is Pickles all right?" Panic for the horse's welfare overwhelmed her.

"She's perfectly fine," Kevin assured her. "She came back to the barn for her breakfast without you. If it weren't for her, we might not have found you as quickly as we did."

"Oh thank God." With a sigh of relief, she shook her head. "I feel like crap."

"You should. It was a nasty fall." His hand reached out and pushed a stray wisp of brown hair from her eyes.

"Emily and Kate came to see you. If anyone asks, I'm your husband and they're your sisters."

"What?"

"They would only allow family in initially. Now we're

stuck with the ruse until you're freed." Kevin sat back and tipped his head to the side. His hair looked disheveled and he was still in sweats. He didn't appear to have shaved, which was fine with her. She thought he was more attractive with a little bit of razor stubble.

"So they were talking about letting you out this afternoon if the doctor thinks you're coherent enough. It was just a bad concussion." He paused as if he was uncomfortable. "I told Emily and Kate I would bring you back to the cottage if you wanted to go back."

"I've overstayed my welcome," she quickly said, now worried that she had been more trouble that he wanted to deal with.

"No, not at all. I just think it might be best for you to reconcile with your friends. Kate, in particular, was very worried about you and very sorry for what transpired between you. If anything bad had happened, she would have blamed herself." He smiled again, this time, it was a hopeful smile. "I could be selfish and want you all to myself, but you did come on holiday with your friends. You should spend some time with them. Perhaps we could all go out together and do things. Your wrist eliminates you from riding any more while you're here."

Her heart sank. That was true. No more riding until her wrist healed, and that wouldn't be until she went home. She didn't want to go home, though. She wanted to stay there, in Ireland, with Kevin MacClery. But that wasn't realistic, was it?

"You look so sad. Don't worry, the horses aren't going anywhere. You'll be good as new in a few months and then we can go riding again." He chuckled.

This time, she felt a surge of joy. He didn't want her to go either. "Yes, but you forget I'm leaving soon."

"Yes, in order to go back to work and sort things out at home, and then you'll have to come back. I'll send a plane ticket for you. Of course, next time, you'll have to stay a month. We can go to Dublin for a week and stay in my apartment there." He seemed to have given the entire situation a lot of thought.

"Sounds decadent." With a contented smile, she closed her eyes and breathed in deeply. His cologne reached her nostrils and she marveled at how much she loved his smell.

He appeared to like that she liked his plan, then he reached out and took her hand again. "I am so relieved you're going to be all right."

"Me too," she agreed. "You're right, I should make things right with Kate. I knew she was just saying hurtful things because her feelings were hurt. I just need to remember not to leave her out."

"Perhaps one night before you all head home we should have a dinner party at my house and we can invite Aedan and Sean as well. That Sean seems to be a respectable bloke, and he likes science fiction. He's also quite keen on your friend Emily."

Sarah smiled and narrowed her eyes. "Good. Emily needs a good man in her life to show her not all men are bastards like her ex."

Kevin smiled at that.

They both turned when they heard Kate's voice at the door. "Hello?"

"Hey Kate, come in," Sarah greeted.

Kate stepped into the room as if she was uncertain about something, but then Emily came in behind her, nodding at someone in the hall.

"Well, it looks like you're being sprung here in a while." Emily sounded upbeat. Her skin looked fresh like she'd had a good night's sleep.

"Oh good, I don't like hospitals." Truthfully, this was the first hospital she'd ever been in. The first thirty years of her life had been enjoyed injury and illness free.

"Hopefully, they give you good drugs for the wrist," Kate said. "I sprained my wrist once and it hurt pretty badly. I can't even imagine a fracture."

Sarah just nodded.

"Do you remember us being here yesterday afternoon?" Em asked.

"Not really. Everything is a bit foggy. I remember talking to a doctor and Kevin, but…" She shrugged.

Kate stepped up to the side of the bed. She wore a bright green, garish shirt. "Then I'm going to have to repeat my apology."

Sarah shook her head this time. "The only thing you have to apologize for is that lime green shirt. Where did you get that?"

Emily laughed, and Kate looked down at the shirt.

Kevin shook his head. "I'm going to get some soda or something. Do any of you want anything?"

"I'd like some tea," Sarah told him, then looked at her friends. Kate and Emily wanted coffee, and so Kevin left, on a mission to acquire beverages for all of them. Sarah knew he just left to give her time with her friends.

"When we get home if you're hungry, we still have leftovers from the dinner Aedan made us last night," Kate said, excited.

"Hmm. How is Aedan?" Sarah gave Emily a knowing look. It was pretty obvious Kate liked the guy.

"He's just a friend. We are going to the same conference in France next month." It was a quick, almost defensive answer, and so Kate-like. "Besides, I'm not the one who had a one-night stand with Sean."

She felt her jaw drop as her attention moved to Emily, whose cheeks began to glow a bright crimson. "Sean? Em, right on."

"It wasn't a one-night stand," Emily corrected, shooting Kate a warning look. "It wasn't that cheap or tawdry."

"So you're going to sleep with him again," Kate said matter-of-factly.

Sarah laughed even though it made her head throb. "Wait, what about," Kate looked around to make sure no one was within earshot, "Kevin?"

"Well we didn't get naked if that's what you're asking, but there's potential. He wants to have all of us up to his house for a dinner party before we leave, and in a few months, I might be coming back for a month, at which time we'll stay in Dublin."

Emily's expression crossed somewhere between happy and surprised. "That's fantastic. I have to say I'm a little jealous."

Kate's smile was even bigger. She was such a hyperactive ball of emotions that Sarah expected a bigger response, but Kate said nothing.

"I know it seems sudden," she directed at Kate. "But the reality is that the first day I met Kevin we just clicked and there was a connection. I don't know if it's going to turn into anything serious, but I have to follow it and see where it goes. If it doesn't, nothing is lost. We've had some good times, but if there's even the slightest chance that I've found another man to spend the rest of my life with, I have to take that chance. I know I don't *need* a man to make me happy, but until Kevin, I didn't realize I could *want* to have another partner in life after Eric. I owe it to myself and Kevin to at least see where this goes."

Kate's eyes brimmed with tears and she leaned down and gave Emily a hug. "I know. I want you to be happy and if Kevin makes you happy, then I agree, you should follow your heart. I support you in anything you do."

"We both do," Emily agreed. Then she paused and pulled out her phone. "Wait, let me get a picture of this momentous event! The time Sarah fractured her wrist in Ireland. We're going to laugh about this when we're old and gray."

Kate wiped her eyes and leaned in next to Sarah and Sarah put on a big smile for the camera. Emily smiled in triumph when she got the shot she wanted, then she sent it to Lucy and her mom for safe-keeping.

Her phone dinged almost immediately. "Is it your mom or Lucy?" Sarah asked.

Emily held back a laugh. "Lucy, she says to tell you that she hopes you heal quickly and that Kate's green shirt is hideous."

Sarah laughed, and Kate pouted. It was likely that green shirt would find its way to the donation pile sooner rather than later.

It took forever for Sarah to be released. Or it felt that way. At least in that sense, hospitals didn't operate any differently in Ireland. Thankfully Kevin had brought her a change of clothes for the ride home. While Kate and Emily drove back to the cottage in the rental, Kevin took Sarah in his car.

"I can bring your suitcases back tonight. I'll have Beth put them together."

Sarah nodded in agreement. "I hope you don't mind."

"Not at all. Besides, you're coming out for a month next

time and I'll have you all to myself. I can be as selfish as I like

with your time if you'll let me." He was excited about their new plan and she could hear it on the edge of his voice and see it in the way his eyes danced when he talked about it.

"It's a deal."

They talked about their planned excursion all the way to the cottage, and before he left, they kissed like lovers who were parting for the first time.

Then he left and she went inside to find Kate and Emily dressed in pajamas.

"Surprise! Low key movie night!" Kate, rather pleased with herself, held the television remote. "We have leftover dinner from last night, cookies, milk, tea, soda, and popcorn."

Emily pointed toward the bedrooms. "I have an extra pair of pajamas in on your bed."

Sarah rushed to her friends, her arms outstretched and embraced them both with a hug.

Just then Emily's phone received another text message.

She pulled back and watched Emily pull out her phone. "Lucy again?"

"And Mom."

"Are we still debating the merits of Kate's shirt?" Kate scoffed. "I'm giving it away, okay?"

Emily snickered. "No, we're planning a family vacation to Ireland."

"We still have two more weeks." Now Sarah was confused. It was amazing how out-of-the-loop one could become in a few days.

"Sean already gave us the dates this summer the cottage would be free. It would be perfect here for Mom to write, and Lucy would have a blast..." Emily's voice trailed off as she read what was on the screen.

"A long distance relationship?" It didn't seem Emily's style, but Sarah was impressed. Emily Frost's heart had thawed. After twelve years of Sam, she deserved it.

"Yeah. It could work," she said. "Besides, Lucy and Mom will have fun. It's a win-win."

"What about work?" Kate asked. Kate and Sarah were lucky to enjoy jobs that allowed for travel and working from wherever they were. Emily, on the other hand, was not.

"I might just look for something more flexible. Besides, I have some money saved up and my mom has suggested more than once I do some freelance copy-editing. I can do that from anywhere." She gave her friends a stealth grin.

"Watch out world, the old-school Emily is in the house," Kate said, in full-blown street-speak.

Sarah laughed. This was more like the pre-Sam Emily she knew back in college. "Let me get changed while you guys cue up the movie. What are we watching anyway?"

"It's a surprise," came Kate's voice down the hall after her.

A deep warmth filled her. Emily found Sean and fell in love and now she was planning a trip back to introduce Sean to her family. Kate had a budding relationship with Aedan, whom she'd see at a conference in France a month from now. And Sarah, she had Kevin and the promise of a new life and new adventure ahead. No one could ever replace Eric, but she could be happy again, and that's all she ever wanted. She went back to her room and put on Emily's pajamas. There was one more reason she felt truly blessed — she did have the best friends a girl could have.

ABOUT THE AUTHOR

 S. J. Reisner began writing at the age of ten and never stopped. Because she loves to read everything, picking a genre didn't come easy. This is why she has four different pen names and writes everything from non-fiction to horror to contemporary romance. Her non-fiction and erotic romances have been bestsellers on Barnes & Noble and Amazon. Under S. J. Reisner she writes general fiction, contemporary romances, adventure fantasy, and YA paranormal stories. This is her first published contemporary romance novel. When she's not writing you can find her herding cats, wrangling vegetables in the garden, or engaging in one of her many hobbies. She lives along the front range of the Rocky Mountains with her husband and two rescue cats. To learn more visit www.sjreisner.com

Books from 5 Prince Publishing
www.5princebooks.com

Saving Sarah May *S.J. Reisner*
Walker Pride *Bernadette Marie*
Abandoned Soul *Doug Simpson*
Copper Lake *Ann Swann*
Grace After the Storm *Sandy Sinnett*
Throne of Jelzicar/Warriors of Gravenlea *S.D. Galloway*
Fatal Desire *Christina OW*
Unwrap the Romance Anthology
The Grand Dissolute *Joel Van Valin*
An Ill Wind *James Hanley*
Stargazing *Bernadette Marie*
Old Amarillo *Sara Barnard*
Nobody's Business *M.J. Kane*
Walker Pride *Bernadette Marie*
A Secret to Keep *Railyn Stone*
The Doom of Undal *Katrina Sisowath*
Fatal Obsession *Christina OW*
The Escape Clause *Bernadette Marie*
Reasons to Stay *Lisa J. Hobman*
Permanent Spring Showers *Scott D. Southard*
Wings *Pete Abela*
Reason to Leave *Lisa J. Hobman*
Love Finds its Way *Wilhelmina Stolen*
The Paper Masque *Jessica Dall*
The Silver Unicorn *Wayne Orr*
The Merger *Bernadette Marie*
Braving the Darkness *Melynda Price*
The Calling *Jim Hanley*
The Christmas Tree Guy *Railyn Stone*